Daniel Putnam

Twenty-Five Years with the Insane

Daniel Putnam

Twenty-Five Years with the Insane

ISBN/EAN: 9783337366094

Printed in Europe, USA, Canada, Australia, Japan

Cover: Foto ©Andreas Hilbeck / pixelio.de

More available books at **www.hansebooks.com**

TWENTY-FIVE YEARS

—WITH—

THE INSANE.

By DANIEL PUTNAM,

LATE CHAPLAIN OF MICHIGAN ASYLUM, AT KALAMAZOO.

DETROIT:

JOHN MACFARLANE.

1885.

PREFATORY NOTE.

The author desires, in this way, to acknowledge his obligations to the Superintendents of the asylums for the insane in Michigan, and especially to Dr. PALMER, of Kalamazoo, for his kindness in examining the manuscript of the book, and for many valuable suggestions. It should be stated, however, that he is in no degree responsible for any opinions and ideas expressed.

It is deemed necessary to make only this general acknowledgment for the material derived from historical and other books treating of mental diseases, since those works are well known to all familiar with the literature of insanity, and most of the matter thus obtained is, to a large extent, common property.

The author is under much obligation to H. A. FORD, Esq., for his invaluable assistance in the corrections of proofs, and for many typographical suggestions.

Messrs. WINN & HAMMOND also deserve grateful mention for the beautiful form in which the book appears.

CONTENTS.

TWENTY-FIVE YEARS WITH THE INSANE.

CHAPTER I.

INTRODUCTORY AND PERSONAL.

The Michigan Asylum for the Insane, at Kalamazoo, was opened in August, 1859. A little later in that year I was invited by the Medical Superintendent, Dr. Van Deusen, to conduct the first religious service held in the institution. This was the beginning of a connection with the asylum which continued for five-and-twenty years. Consequently, during a large part of an ordinary lifetime I have been brought into somewhat intimate relation with the insane, and with the officers of an institution which may justly claim to rank among the very best in the country. These many years have given abundant opportunities for observing many varieties of mental disease, and for learning whatever an unprofessional observer might be able to learn. One would be indeed beyond hope of forgiveness if nothing of value to himself and others were gathered up with such facilities.   I have a desire, if possible, to render this knowledge of some practical service to parents, teachers, students, and others employed in the common pursuits and business of every-day life.   It is for this reason, chiefly, that I write these chapters.

I wish, at the outset, to guard against a possible misconception of the nature and character of the book.   It is not necessary to say that I do not write as a physician or a specialist, because that would be readily understood.   It might, however, on account of the position which I have occupied, not unnaturally be supposed that I have studied and observed as a clergyman, and that I speak as a member of that honored profession.   I count it, on the whole, a fortunate thing that I am only a layman, authorized by the custom of the religious organization with which I am connected to conduct the exercises of social and public worship.   My duties as a teacher have brought me constantly, for more than thirty years, into daily contact with young, healthy, and vigorous mental and physical life.   The means have, therefore, been at hand for comparing, at pleasure and day by day, normal and morbid mental activity.   If one had desired, it would have been impossible to avoid such comparison, or to forbear drawing from it lessons for the school-room and the home.   I write, consequently, especially as a teacher, and as a student, in a very humble way, of the science of mind, in which professional duties have required me to give instruction.

I do not speak upon the subject of insanity as an expert. I wish distinctly and emphatically to disclaim any such purpose. I have neither the knowledge nor the inclination necessary to enable me to do a work of that kind. Besides, perfect candor impels the confession that observation, both within and without the asylum, leads me to estimate at a very moderate value the opinions of the majority of self-constituted experts. I can not resist the conviction that so-called expert testimony has been the occasion, if not the cause, of much harm to the worthy and honest insane, both in the courts and elsewhere.

Having thus guarded against misapprehension in one direction, it may be allowable to say a word in relation to the position and duties of a chaplain in an asylum for the insane, as they appear in the light of experience and reflection. The impression is doubtless general, that the chaplain of an institution of any kind is an officer charged with duties mainly, if not exclusively, religious in their character. It is supposed, not unnaturally, that he has to do almost exclusively with the moral and spiritual condition of the inmates, and that in this sphere he should have the right to act with entire freedom from the control or direction of any superior. Any interference, by dictation or by very earnest suggestion, with his purposes, plans, or methods of labor, would be considered by some persons as an infringement upon prerogative, if not upon the province of conscience itself.

This view of the position and rights of a chaplain may be correct, for aught I know, in institutions where inmates are free from any irregular activity, either of the intellect or the emotions.

But experience and observation have gradually brought me to the conviction that this officer can not occupy such a position of independence and self-direction in an asylum for the insane with safety to the general interests of the institution, or with advantage to the inmates themselves, unless he possesses unusual soundness of judgment, great prudence and discretion, and much practical knowledge of insanity and the insane. This conclusion has not been reached hastily, nor as a result of any expressions of opinion on the part of the medical superintendents or other officers with whom I have been associated. During five-and-twenty years I received no dictation, no unpleasant or undesired suggestions, and no restraint of any kind upon liberty of speech or action. Yet I am sure my mistakes would have been much more frequent and serious, in personal intercourse with patients, but for wise and timely counsel given in the most delicate and oftentimes indirect manner.

In his general duties the chaplain is not a pastor in the common acceptation of that term. The ordinary methods of a pastor, transferred to the halls of an asylum, might easily work untold evil. In the public services of the chapel the differences are much less. The general truths of the gospel may be spoken with ordinary freedom and plainness. It will only be necessary to avoid exciting topics and exciting manners and methods. It hardly needs to be suggested that the distinctive doctrines and peculiarities of sects and parties would be sadly out of place in ministering to such an audience.

It is in the direct personal intercourse of the chaplain with patients that he finds the need of peculiar wisdom and discretion. In this intercourse, with the best of intentions, it will be easy to inflict much injury, and to hinder the progress of recovery. To a large extent, religious truth and religious instruction and exhortation appeal to the emotional nature. In many, perhaps in a majority of cases, especially among females, mental disease touches directly or indirectly this part of the nature. It will not be difficult, in cases of this sort, to excite a morbid and harmful degree of emotional activity. This intensity of feeling, of whatever nature it may be, produces unfavorable results upon the nervous system, prevents rest, and tends to create irritability and even maniacal excitement. This illustration will be sufficient to indicate some of the difficulties to be met, and the necessity of receiving advice and counsel from the medical officers who have carefully studied the peculiar conditions of individual inmates. Religious services and religious reading or conversation are, at some times and in some circumstances, the occasion, if not the cause, of much suffering and evil to individuals. And not unfrequently such persons have a very strong desire for such reading and conversation. The chaplain will very likely be reproached for apparently neglecting these patients, and the officers in charge will be accused of cruelty for refusing permission to attend church or chapel exercises.

The inquiry has frequently been made of me by those not familiar with the interior life of an asylum for the insane, whether the services of a chaplain can be of any real value to the inmates of such an institution. My present position will enable me to express an opinion upon this question free from the supposed influence of personal interest.

The inquiry comes, in most cases, from persons who do not know, or fail to keep in mind, the widely differing classes of inmates and the numerous varieties of mental disease. Patients suffering from complete dementia, or from violent attacks of acute mania, are, for the time, beyond the reach of instruction or of human consolation by any direct communication of mind with mind by ordinary religious services. But among almost all other classes of inmates there are very many individuals who receive, directly or indirectly, I believe, great benefit from personal conversation and from the chapel services. Not a few of these are members of churches. They have been accustomed to attend public and social worship. Such periods of devotion and instruction have become an important part of their conception of life and duty. When these can not be enjoyed, the loss is deeply and sorely felt, though it may not be very clearly understood or expressed. The condition is like that of which most of us have been conscious, at one time or another: something is wanting,—we may not be able to tell what,—but there is a feeling of vague and distressing unrest which prevents all contentment and repose of mind. This unrest is a great obstacle to recovery, especially when the power of self-control has been lost or seriously weakened.

Moreover, many patients suffer from mild or periodic forms of mental disorder. Excepting at intervals of greater or less frequency, they are in possession of a good degree of intellectual strength. In addition to these, there are always persons nearly or quite restored to their usual degree of health, waiting for time to give confirmed vigor both of body and mind.

To both these classes all truths have a familiar and accustomed sound. The forms of worship, the tones of prayer, the songs of praise, words of instruction and exhortation and comfort, are to them the same here as elsewhere. By such well-known and often highly prized services, assurance is constantly given that they are not cast out from friendly and Christian society and from personal and Christian sympathy, although sundered from home and the ordinary relationships and associations of life. In some cases this is a potent factor in stimulating effort to recover self-control, and in keeping the soul from sinking into apathy, if not into despair. In this and in other ways, the chaplaincy, entirely apart from any considerations of a moral and religious character, takes an important place among the so-called moral means of curing or alleviating insanity. It is quite possible that its highest value is found here. I am persuaded also that its good influence often reaches even to the disturbed and demented patients. The sympathizing and comforting utterances of the " Man of Sorrows," falling upon ears accustomed elsewhere and under happier circumstances to listen to them, are like sweet strains of music heard long ago and dimly and faintly remembered. They convey little conscious instruction or consolation, and may hardly be retained until the brief service is ended. But even thus they are not altogether worthless. The attention has been caught and held for a moment; the memory has been half awakened, and has groped for an instant amid the mental darkness after the forgotten. Over the vacant face and into the dull eyes, has flashed a single gleam of returning intelligence. Down into the brooding gloom has fallen one ray of blessed light, and, for a brief interval, the marvelous grasp of some strange, strong delusion has been loosened. A little gleam of coming hope has

faintly illumined the darkness of the present. There
has been a little ray of blessed sunlight through
the clouds. An existence which, to an observer,
seems only a grievous burden, has been made tolerable, at least for a passing moment.

These introductory and personal considerations
may find a fitting close in some statements concerning the number of patients who have been under
treatment since my connection with the asylum
began. At the time of the first religious service,
only a small portion of one wing of the original
building had been completed, and only females
had been admitted. The number of patients
was but thirty-one, and the whole population connected with the place was scarcely fifty
persons. On the first of October of this year (1884),
the number of patients was seven hundred and nine-
ty-eight, and the whole resident population more
than nine hundred. During these twenty-five years
3859 patients have been received. Of this large
number, nine hundred and thirty-six have been discharged as restored to usual health, and seven
hundred and seventy as more or less improved.

The Eastern Asylum at Pontiac has been opened for
six years and two months. On the first of October,
1884, it had six hundred and fifty-three patients.
Since its opening it has admitted 1474, and discharged as cured two hundred and fifty-six, and as
improved two hundred and seventy-eight.

Up to October 1, 1884, both asylums have admitted 5333 patients, and have discharged as restored 1182, and as improved 1048.

These figures have, in one direction, an aspect of peculiar and inexpressible sadness. They stand, in many cases, for homes darkened and the most tender ties rudely broken. Though silent, they speak of a vast amount of human suffering and sorrow, and of suffering and sorrow in forms which have hitherto received less than a just share of pity and sympathy and consideration.

In another aspect they afford a little light amid the general gloom, a little sunshine in spite of the clouds. The shadows remain, but they are much relieved. Many who came to the asylum sick in mind and body, have departed "clothed and in their right minds." Hundreds of homes, scattered over the State, have been made "exceeding glad" by the return of a father or mother, a brother or sister, a child or a companion. It has been permitted me to see not a few come up out of the deepest darkness of mental and sometimes spiritual night, into the blessed daylight of hope and joy and peace. Some such I have been allowed to meet in their own homes, filled with overflowing gratitude and thankfulness.

What I have seen and heard has left a firm conviction in my mind that asylums and hospitals for the insane have done much for the relief of one of the most pitiable forms of human suffering. I believe it is possible for these institutions to do more and better in the future. Improvements in means and methods are to be expected in these, as in all other human institutions. During the present century wonderful progress has been made in many directions. Much, doubtless, still remains to be accomplished.

To show what has already been done, I have introduced several short historical chapters, the matter of which is borrowed and condensed from various authors, to whom I desire in this way to give all due credit.

Observation has also impressed me with the belief that much insanity might be prevented. This is true, I suppose, of most forms of disease, but it seems to me to be peculiarly true in respect to mental disorders. The opinion is very general that insanity has been for many years, and still is, increasing. While I do not think the rate of increase is so great as census reports appear to indicate, it is yet evidently sufficient to justify alarm, and to call for serious inquiry into the causes and for means of prevention. The object of the later chapters is to turn the thoughts of parents, teachers, and others who are especially responsible for the training of the young, in that direction.

CHAPTER II.

INSANITY AND ITS TREATMENT AMONG THE ANCIENTS.

Our knowledge of insanity among the earliest historical peoples is very limited and unsatisfactory. Incidental allusions in the oldest preserved writings, both sacred and secular, indicate that the disease manifested itself, at least occasionally, even in the ages of primitive civilization and habits. Everything which may be said as to the probable frequency of such manifestations is pure conjecture, based upon supposed conditions of society, modes of life, and employments.

The legislation of Moses makes no mention of lunacy, but references are found in the Hebrew Scriptures to forms of madness which were obviously attacks of insanity. King Saul undoubtedly suffered from periodical outbursts of some species of mental disorder. His conduct on several occasions can be explained on no other hypothesis. His jealousy, irritability, and unreasoning acts of violence exhibit peculiarities readily recognized by those who are familiar with the behavior of insane men. The employment of music for the relief of Saul, when seized by these paroxysms, enables us to discover one of the means used for the cure or mitigation of insanity in that age.

David, when his life was in danger at the court of Achish, feigned madness. This instance of assumed imbecility, for such seems to have been the type of David's insanity, has a twofold interest. It justifies us in concluding that cases of real imbecility were so frequent as to fall under general observation. David could not have simulated successfully conduct with which he had not a tolerably good acquaintance; and King Achish would not, at once, have pronounced him mad if he had not often seen madmen before. The inference is unavoidable that some forms of insanity were common in that part of the ancient East.

The case of David throws light also upon the probable treatment of the insane among the Hebrews and Philistines. Among them, as among some other nations of antiquity, it seems evident that a certain degree of respect and reverence was felt for persons afflicted with some types of madness. They were believed to have been touched by the finger of some divinity, and to be under his protection and guidance. They were, in some cases, supposed to be partially inspired and to be able to utter oracles. In other cases, they were believed to be suffering special punishment, inflicted directly and immediately by a deity. Consequently, to lay human hands on them in violence was impiety, and might bring divine vengeance down upon the head of the offender.

Where such feelings and opinions prevailed, the mild and harmless insane were allowed to go at large, and were hedged about with a sort of invisible but efficient protection. David's pretended madness, therefore, was sure to afford him temporary security from any serious ill-treatment, and to give him opportunity to make his escape. The violently insane were without doubt at that time, as they certainly were at a later period among the Jews, confined with fetters and chains.

The condition of the insane in other countries of the ancient East seems to have been essentially the same as in Syria and Palestine. Nebuchadnezzar suffered, for seven years, from an attack of that form of lunacy which is now known as lycanthropia or lycanthropy. This species of insanity is not uncommon, and under its influence the poor victim imagines himself to be a beast, and behaves, as far as possible, like the animal into which he believes he has been transformed. If the mightiest monarch of the time, while laboring under a most pitiable delusion, was turned out to wander over the fields with the cattle, to eat grass like the ox, to go with uncut nails and uncombed hair and beard, to be unsheltered and totally neglected, it is not difficult to determine the amount and kind of care and consideration bestowed upon the insane in Babylonia and in the other great Oriental kingdoms.

In Egypt, and also in Greece, it is said that some temples, dedicated to the worship of certain deities, were open for the admission of persons of disordered intellects. If this were so, the practice probably originated in the belief that insanity was caused by the direct purpose and act of some agency higher than man. It is, moreover, affirmed by a few writers, but upon questionable authority, that some of the most enlightened of the Greek physicians employed humane and scientific remedies in their treatment of insanity. As a rule, in Egypt, Greece, and Italy, the insane fared no better than in the East. Everywhere they were treated with abuse or neglect. If inoffensive, they were permitted to wander at will; if violent and dangerous, they were loaded with chains and fetters.

Hospitals and asylums were unknown in the old world. Near the temples of Æsculapius, the god of medicine and patron of physicians, houses were sometimes built for the reception of visitors who came to seek advice and direction of the deity, either for themselves or for suffering friends. But these were merely places of shelter and refuge, and not hospitals, in the modern acceptation of the name, where medical care and attendance could be had. Organized charities, either of a public or private character, for the support or relief of the aged, the unfortunate, the destitute, the sick, the blind, or the insane, had no place in the civilizations which preceded the Christian era.

CHAPTER III.

THE INSANE DURING THE EARLY CHRISTIAN CENTURIES.

In the olden times men loved their families, their friends, their neighbors, and, in a less degree, their countrymen. The feelings of pity and compassion existed in their souls. The impulses of good-will, and benevolence, and charity were not wanting. But love, and pity, and charity were confined within very narrow bounds. Strangers were enemies, and enemies might be hated and killed without blame. Men were not regarded, protected, or cared for, simply because they were men. The great majority "went by on the other side" of wounded and bleeding humanity, unless the kinship was very close and the tax upon resources and effort was very light.

The "Galilean" imposed "a new commandment" upon his followers, and emphasized, if He did not introduce, a new principle of human action. His disciples were to "love one another," not because they were of kindred blood, not because they were friends, neighbors, or countrymen; but because they were of one common humanity, children of the same divine Father. There was to be in His kingdom no Jew nor Gentile, no Greek nor Barbarian, no bond nor free, but only citizens and brethren.

Moreover, the love, or charity, of the new com-, mandment was intensely practical in its character. It was not a mere emotion or sentiment. It was not to find expression in words alone. In deeds it was to be embodied and manifested. The hungry were to be fed, the naked were to be clothed, the sick were to be healed. Blind eyes were to be opened, deaf ears were to be unstopped, lepers were to be cleansed, and demons to be cast out. These works of benef- icence and mercy were to be done in all lands and for all peoples.

The first manifestations of Christian charity were unorganized. Individuals helped, according to their means and opportunities, other individuals. Then small local bodies helped the poor and unfortunate immediately about them. Gradually the work became reduced to system and order by the union of these local societies over a considerable extent of territory. As means increased, hospitals and other public recep- tacles for the needy, the sick, and the suffering began, for the first time in the history of the world, to be built and opened to persons of all classes and creeds.

The first hospital is said to have been erected by a Christian woman in Rome in the fourth Christian century. Soon after, others were founded in all the great centers of the Roman empire. Asylums were established for lepers, for blind beggars, for the infirm and aged, indeed, for almost every form of misfortune and misery. The church in Antioch, in the time of

2

St. Chrysostom, besides caring for the sick and strangers, supported three thousand widows and young girls. About the same period the church in Rome provided for fifteen hundred widows and other indigent persons, at an expense of not less than eighteen thousand dollars a year. Other churches, in other great cities, engaged with equal zeal in the same work of charity and mercy. A single collection in Carthage for the ransom of prisoners yielded four thousand dollars, although the Christians in that city were neither numerous nor wealthy. The laws of the new societies made it the duty of the officers and overseers "to take care for the maintenance of all who were in distress, and to let none of them want; to supply to orphans the care of parents, to widows the care of husbands, to help to marriage those ready for marriage, to procure work for those out of work, to show compassion to those incapable of work, to provide a shelter for strangers, food for the hungry, drink for the thirsty, visits for the sick, and help for the prisoners."

In all this grand development of practical love, charity, and benevolence, the grandest which the world has ever seen, the insane seem to have found no remembrance, or, if any, so little that it has escaped the notice of all historians. Those bereft of sight were sheltered and fed; those more sorely bereft of reason were left to go homeless and hungry. Lepers, though types of physical and moral uncleanness, shared a charity which was denied to the maniac. This apparent inconsistency can not be explained on the supposition that the insane were so few as to be overlooked, or that their sufferings were so inconsiderable as to need no relief and to make no appeal to the feelings of pity and compassion. The mystery finds its probable solution in quite another direction.

The ancient belief that the insane were influenced by spiritual agencies, and were, in some way, peculiarly related to superhuman powers, has already been alluded to. Nearly allied to this doctrine was the belief in witchcraft and demoniacal possession. The early Christians received these beliefs by natural inheritance, and they have been perpetuated, by tradition and by an intuitive tendency of the human mind towards the strange and marvelous, down to a period within the memory of some now living. Moreover, the sacred writings, both of the Old and New Testaments, as usually and most literally interpreted, seemed to teach that demons could and did, by some means, enter into the human body, if not into the soul. Probably the most generally accepted doctrine of the present day, among those who adhere to a pretty literal interpretation of the Scriptures, is that such power of possession, once permitted to demons, was limited to certain peculiar periods, conditions, and circumstances, and has not been extended indefinitely into the Christian centuries. The members and teachers of the early churches saw no reason for supposing such limitation. Demons and other infernal powers were as mighty, and as much to be dreaded, hated, and resisted in the fourth, and even in the seventeenth, as in the first centuries. To express a doubt of the reality of witchcraft was to expose one's self to the charge of Sadduceeism.

Now, many of the external manifestations of acute mania and epilepsy bear a most marked resemblance to the conduct of persons who were believed to be possessed. Consequently maniacs, and those of the insane laboring under many delusions, could not be distinguished from demoniacs. It was not unnatural, therefore, that the fear, distrust, and detestation felt towards men and women believed to be in most intimate association with evil spirits, or even to be inhabited by demons, should be turned towards the unfortunate victims of insanity, since the two classes had, apparently, so many characteristics in common. Here, without much reasonable doubt, is found the true cause why, through many sad and desolate ages, the insane were left almost entirely outside the widely extended arms of human and Christian charity. They received hatred in place of love. They were punished rather than pitied. Scourges, chains, and fetters were given them instead of food, and medicine, and shelter. Occasionally the older belief that the harmless and inoffensive insane were inspired and protected by the Deity and by good spirits, secured special favor and peculiar consideration for certain

classes of lunatics, and certain forms of lunacy.
During the confusions, and disorders, and violence of
the times when society seemed resolving itself into its
original elements, many more fled away from the
cities and towns, and dwelt alone in caves and in
other wild and secluded places. In the warm climate of the East and South nature demanded but
little clothing. Their garments were of the coarsest
and rudest kind, and their food simple and scanty.
Personal cleanliness was not esteemed among the
virtues, and their hair and beard were allowed to
grow long and shaggy. In many cases, advancing
years gave them a sort of rustic dignity, and common
opinion ascribed to them peculiar sanctity and
wisdom.

Living thus apart, with little human intercourse,
with no books, possessed with the generally received
belief that evil spirits frequented the wilderness and
deserts, they easily fell into an unbalanced state of
mind. They became subject to hallucinations and
delusions. They had struggles and contests with
demons. They were visited, helped, and comforted
by good angels. They saw and heard most marvelous things. Coming occasionally out of their wild
retreats, they wandered over the country, and through
the streets of villages and cities. They were received
with great respect and reverence, not only by the
common people, but by the clergy and by others in
high places of influence and authority. Their disor-

dered fancies were accepted, to a considerable extent, as veritable accounts of actual occurrences, and were embodied and preserved in the legends and lives of saints. Insane persons of this class, and of a few other kindred classes, were treated, not indeed wisely, but with humanity and kindness. Whatever sufferings they endured were self-inflicted. For once credulity and superstition performed the offices of compassion and charity.

Equally harmless and innocent victims of other forms of insane delusion were less fortunate. In place of reverence and tenderness, they were treated with punishments, and tortures, and death. It is not uncommon now for insane men and women to imagine themselves to be divine personages. Such delusions are not considered, at the present day, more dangerous or more blameworthy than a thousand others. In earlier centuries less lenient views were entertained of such vagaries of diseased minds. They were believed to involve the sin of impiety and blasphemy, and to deserve the heaviest penalties and the most cruel torments, both here and hereafter. To pity or spare such monsters of wickedness was to incur a degree of guilt hardly less than their own. The mercy of a peaceful and painless death was denied them. Two or three examples will show the temper of the times.

"In the year 1300, a beautiful English girl appeared at Milan, laboring under the delusion that she was the Holy Ghost, incarnated for the redemption of women." Instead of finding pity and refuge in an asylum, she suffered death by fire. A Spaniard, declaring himself to be a brother of the archangel Michael, and affirming that he was to occupy the high position in heaven which Satan had forfeited and lost, was burned alive by the command of the Archbishop of Toledo. The death of Joan of Arc affords another illustration of native barbarism intensified by political and religious hate. Great numbers of the common people perished, year by year, after having been exposed to every conceivable species of insult and torture. The phenomena and treatment of mediæval and modern witchcraft, so-called, present a marvelous admixture of honest credulity, of wicked deception, of heartless and fiendish cruelty, and of the illusions and delusions of insanity. The insane shared the hatred and fate of the wicked.

CHAPTER IV.

THE FIRST HOSPITALS AND ASYLUMS FOR THE INSANE, AND THEIR CHARACTER.

In the sixth century a house of shelter or refuge is said to have been opened at Jerusalem for insane monks. Amid the turmoil of that period large numbers of these monks were wandering over the East.

So far as now known, no hospital or asylum for the insane existed in Europe till after the year 1400.

In 1409, a man of humane spirit observed the rabble following and hooting at some maniacs in the streets of the city of Valencia, in Spain. Moved with compassion, he secured the erection of a house into which they might be received and protected from insult and abuse. In 1425, an asylum was founded in Saragossa; in 1436, others in Seville and Valladolid, and one in Toledo in 1483. Previous to this time the Mohammedans had made some organized provision for the insane among them. A writer of the seventh century states that several buildings were erected for lunatics in Fez, in which the more violent were confined in chains. It is reported that a hospital was founded in Cairo in 1304. Doubtless receptacles existed in other Mohammedan cities. Of the military orders, the Knights of Malta alone admitted insane patients into their hospitals. An asylum was built at Rome in 1548, and gradually receptacles were opened in all the countries of Europe.

In England the first house of a public, or semi-public, character established for the insane, was Bethlehem Hospital, in London. Some shadows of doubt and uncertainty have gathered about the origin of this institution. Statements put forth by different writers do not harmonize with each other. The hospital seems to have been founded, about

1247, as a priory, or place of refuge, for the religious order of St. Mary of Bethlehem. There is no satisfactory evidence of the admission of insane patients until about the year 1400. At that time, in consequence of some misbehavior of an officer, a royal commission examined into the condition of the hospital. Their report disclosed the fact that six men, who were lunatics, were found there, and the inventory of furniture and other appurtenances includes "six chains of iron, with six locks, four pairs of manacles of iron, and two pairs of stocks." These articles are only too suggestive of the treatment to which the unfortunate inmates were probably subjected. The next asylum in England was not opened till 1751, and up to the year 1792 only fifteen hospitals of all kinds for the insane had been established in Great Britain.

It is a matter of grave doubt whether the establishment of these so-called hospitals and asylums improved the condition and treatment of persons afflicted with mental disease. They were perhaps necessary steps along the road of slow progress towards humane and scientific treatment. But they were little else than prisons, and most of them were prisons of the worst description. They were erected and filled, not from considerations of humanity and mercy towards their inmates, but for the protection of society and the relief of relatives and friends. In not a few cases the buildings were absolutely unfit for habita-

tions of the vilest animals, mere gloomy, frightful
dens. Men, and sometimes women, cowered in narrow, cold, damp cells of stone, without light or air,
furnished with only a bed of straw, which was rarely
renewed. In some receptacles the attendants were
convicts from prisons, and the wretched insane were
entirely at their mercy. They were heavily chained
and fettered. Day and night the places echoed with
cries, howlings, and clankings of chains. Not all the
hospitals were so terrible, but even the best of those
days would not now be tolerated for an hour. One
would be glad, for the honor of our common humanity, to tear out and destroy the historic pages upon
which such humiliating records are found; but it is
necessary to recall and open them in order to estimate
justly the rate and character of the progress which
the present century has made in the care and treatment of insanity and the insane.

For many years Bethlem Hospital, or Bedlam, as
it was usually called, was one of the public shows of
London. It was visited for the same reasons, and
with the same feelings and curiosity, with which the
menagerie and the cock-pit were frequented. The
admission fee was one or two pennies, and the income
from this source was sometimes two thousand dollars
annually. Strange to say, this barbarous custom
continued as late as 1770, and, from incidental allusions in English literature, it is evident that all
classes regarded maniacs just as they did caged and

chained wild beasts. Evelyn writes in one place, "I stepped into Bedlam, where I saw several poor creatures in chains; one of them was mad with making verses." Ned Ward, in his "London Spy," gives an extended account of a visit to the place. "We were admitted in through an iron gate, within which sat a brawny Cerberus of an indigo color, leaning upon a money-box; we turned in through another iron barricade, where we heard such a rattling of chains, drumming of doors, ranting, hollowing, singing, and running, that I could think of nothing but Don Quevedo's Vision, where the lost souls broke loose and put hell in an uproar."

In one of his famous pictures in the "Rake's Progress," Hogarth represents two ladies of fashion visiting this hospital while the keeper is putting fetters upon the poor rake. Near by stands a person supposed to be the doctor, and the miserable woman who has followed the rake in his downward course is looking on. A conspicuous figure in the picture is a maniac, lying on straw in one of the cells, with a chain distinctly in view. A man, who imagines himself a king, is seen in another cell, wearing a crown of straw. Several other insane characters can be readily recognized, among them an astronomer, a musician, and a high ecclesiastic. The whole representation has a profound historical interest. Hogarth seems to have drawn from life.

Of medical treatment, in the proper sense of that term, there was none in any of these institutions. Of moral means for restoring "minds diseased," it is difficult to discover that any were employed. Over the portals of these abodes of misery might well have been written, "Who enters here leaves hope behind."

The early history of the treatment of the insane in the United States is little else than a repetition of European history during the same time. Until very late in the colonial period no special provisions were made anywhere in the country for the cure or the comfort of lunatics. No hospitals or asylums existed. The insane wandered abroad, were cared for by friends, or were confined in jails, almshouses, stables, and out-buildings. They endured neglect, abuse, chains, fetters, filth, and frost. Among us, as among all other peoples, exceptional cases received humane and Christian consideration and care; but here, as elsewhere, the great majority suffered without pity and died without consolation. Investigations in New York and in some other States, in the early years of the present century, proved that all the horrors of European receptacles were duplicated in our own jails, poor-houses, and other places of detention, both private and public.

The first hospital into which insane patients were regularly admitted, in the then colonies, was the Pennsylvania General Hospital, opened in 1752. Only a limited number were received. It is claimed,

I hope with truth, that the treatment of the insane in that institution anticipated, in a good degree, the reforms and improvements which began nearly half a century later in France and England. It is certain that the atmosphere of Philadelphia was then thoroughly permeated by the humane and kindly influence of the Society of Friends, and that Dr. Franklin was greatly interested in the establishment and management of this Hospital. The first asylum, exclusively for the insane, was built by the colony of Virginia, in 1773, at Williamsburg. This was established and supported at public expense, and still remains as the Eastern Asylum of that State. Insane patients were received into the hospital at the city of New York as early as 1797. Out of that institution grew the present Bloomingdale asylum, opened in 1821. "The Friends' Asylum, opened for the relief of persons deprived of the use of their reason," was established near Philadelphia in 1817. The McLean asylum at Somerville, near Boston, was opened in 1818. A small asylum was erected by the State of South Carolina, at Columbia, in 1822. The Connecticut Retreat for the Insane, at Hartford, was founded in 1824, and the Kentucky asylum, at Lexington, was established in the same year. Since this last date numerous hospitals and asylums, both public and private, have been founded in all parts of the United States.

CHAPTER V.

CURIOUS SUPERSTITIONS, AND STRANGE METHODS OF TREATING THE INSANE.

Until insanity took its place among recognized diseases of the physical organism, its origin was shrouded in mystery which excited and, at the same time, baffled inquiry and investigation. Its phenomena were so strange, so utterly inexplicable by any known laws of mental action, that, not very unnaturally, the remedies employed for its cure, especially by the ignorant and superstitious, were of the most absurd and irrational character. The use of such means may have had a beginning in some lucky accident, or in some sudden caprice as wild as the vagaries of insanity itself. Once begun, the practice could easily be kept alive. Soon tradition would come in to repeat marvelous tales of its efficacy, and to exaggerate the evidences of its power and virtue. Habits, customs, rites, however fantastic and even repulsive, thoroughly established among a rural and unenlightened people, have great tenacity of life. They survive in spite of the hottest fires of persecution, and the plainest teachings of science and philosophy. Like the seeds of noxious plants, they take root and spring up in the most unexpected places, and under circumstances apparently the most unpropitious. In regard to matters of this kind, our own age, with all its self-laudation, has little reason for casting reproaches upon earlier times.

We can claim for our Saxon ancestors, no more than for our Celtic, any superabundance of either humanity or wisdom in their dealings with the criminal and the unfortunate. The prescriptions of their physicians, educated in the learning of their times, were singular admixtures of castigation, medicine, superstition, and religion. Emetics, cathartics, herbs, and masses were administered with impartial liberality. A man troubled with hallucinations was fed with properly prepared wolf's flesh. Mixtures of ale and holy water were given to possessed persons. Scourgings and chains found frequent use. The moon had influence both upon the disease and upon the efficacy of remedies.

Faith in the curative influence of the waters of certain wells and springs was very wide-spread and long continued. Indeed, this faith, perhaps slightly disturbed and a little weakened, still survives in obscure nooks and corners of the Old World, and possibly in the New. Insane patients were plunged into these waters with appropriate and mystic rites. Into one pool it was prescribed that the victim should be thrown backwards, should be violently tossed up and down by strong attendants until thoroughly exhausted, then conveyed to a church near at hand, that masses might be sung over him. If one experience of this sort did not effect a cure, the treatment was repeated. This method of cure was practiced, in Great Britain, late in the last century.

Scotland has been, probably, more celebrated than any other country for its mind-healing wells and springs. The superstitious observances connected with some of these have hardly yet entirely disappeared. St. Fillan's pool in Perthshire was one of the most famous of these. In "Marmion," Scott makes one of his characters say :—

> "Then to St. Fillan's blessed well,
> Whose spring can frenzied dreams dispel,
> And the crazed brain restore."

Into this pool patients were plunged three times, then securely bound hand and foot, and left alone for the night in a chapel near by. If the poor maniac could contrive to free himself from the cords, his recovery was confidently expected; if he was found still tied, little hope was entertained of his restoration. Sometimes death followed the exhaustion produced by the process, and brought a happy deliverance from troubles.

As recently as 1793, it is stated that "about two hundred persons, afflicted with insanity, were brought to try the salutary influence of these sacred waters annually."

In Ross-shire, on a small island in Loch Maree, is another famous well. Whittier, in his inimitable manner, has sung the virtue of these waters. He says,—

> "Calm on the breast of Loch Maree
> A little isle reposes;
> A shadow, woven of the oak
> And willow, o'er it closes.

> "Within, a Druid's mound is seen,
> Set round with stony warders;
> A fountain, gushing through the turf,
> Flows o'er the grassy borders.

> "And whoso bathes therein his brow,
> With care or madness burning,
> Feels once again his healthful thought
> And sense of peace returning."

Pennant, who visited the spot in 1769, writes, "The curiosity of the place is the well of the saint, of power unspeakable in cases of lunacy. The patient is brought into the sacred island, is made to kneel before the altar, where his attendants leave an offering of money; he is then brought to the well and sips some of the holy water; a second offering is made; that done, he is thrice dipped into the lake, and the same operation is repeated every day for some weeks." Dr. Mitchell, Commissioner of Lunacy in Scotland, in giving an account of this island in 1862, says: "About seven years before (that is, about 1855), a furious madman was brought there. A rope was passed round his waist, and with a couple of men at one end in advance, and a couple at the

3

other behind, like a furious bull to the slaughter-house, he was marched to the Loch side and placed in a boat, which was pulled once round the island, the patient being jerked into the water at intervals. He was then landed, drank of the water, attached his offering to the tree, and, as I was told, in a state of happy tranquillity went home." Performances nearly as absurd and incredible as these are reported, on good authority, to have taken place at some of the Lochs of Scotland within fifteen years.

Ireland can claim to rival its sister kingdom in the abundance and efficacy of its sacred waters. In Kerry is a glen known as the "Valley of the Lunatics," in which are two wells called the "Lunatics' Wells." It was an old tradition, very generally received by the common people, that all the insane in the country, if left to themselves, would find their way to this valley, and that the waters and other mysterious virtues of the glen would restore them to mental soundness. The continental countries of Europe are probably not surpassed by Great Britain in the number and character of their popular traditions and superstitions relating to the relief of mental maladies, and the treatment appropriate to the insane.

Everything among us is comparatively new. We have few lakes, wells, or valleys around which traditions have been able to gather. Besides, the reaction following the witchcraft excitement introduced an era of doubt and caution. Yet superstitious notions and observances, of a somewhat milder and less offensive character, touching the causes and treatment of insanity, might easily be gathered up, which would considerably lessen our native inclination to compare ourselves with the older nations to their disadvantage.

Reference has already been made to remedies anciently employed by physicians of education and intelligence. This point will bear a little additional illustration, which will render the progress of recent years more obvious. In 1542, a London physician, one. Dr. Borde, published a medical work, in which he says, "I do advertise every man the which is mad, or lunatic, or frantic, or demoniac, to be kept in safeguard in some close house or chamber where there is little light; and that he have a keeper the which the mad man do fear." He further directs that no pictures of man or woman be placed upon the walls of the room, and that the patient be not allowed to have any instrument with which he could do himself harm. He is to be shaved once a month, to drink no strong liquor, and to be provided with a simple diet. This doctor was evidently much in advance of his age in his ideas and methods. Allusions in literature indicate a generally received opinion that the insane should be confined in darkened rooms. In "Twelfth Night," Shakespeare makes one of his actors say, "Come, we'll put him in a dark room, and bound. My niece is already in the belief that he is mad." And in "As You Like It," another says,

"Love is merely a madness; and, I tell you, deserves as well a dark house and a whip, as madmen do."

The medical treatment prescribed in Burton's famous work, "The Anatomy of Melancholy," consists mainly in the use of herbs, some to affect the heart, some the head, some the liver, some the stomach, and others to purify the blood. Hellebore is a favorite remedy, as it was among the old Romans.

Another author recommends for epilepsy and lethargy, poultices of figs and mustard applied to the head. Feverfew was said to be "good for such as be melancholy, sad, pensive, and without speech." Bachelors' buttons were prescribed to be "hung in a linen cloth about the neck of him that is lunatic, in the wane of the moon, when the sign shall be in the first degree of Taurus or Scorpio."

An intimate connection was believed to exist between the liver and insanity, and hence it was of much importance "to get rid of the black bile." For this purpose purges, emetics, bleeding, issues, and shaving the head were advised. "A choice balsam of earth-worms or bats" was recommended for anointing the backbone.

The belief in witchcraft as one of the most common and virulent causes of insanity colored the medical as well as the legal practice of many centuries. Burton recognized this as active in producing melancholy. Coke and Hale recognized it in the conclusions and decisions of the courts of law. King James I. was violently angry with Reginald Scot for daring to oppose the prevalent belief, and for affirming that proper medicines and wholesome diet were more needed than tortures and punishments.

The treatment thus far described was that given outside the so-called hospitals and asylums. The practice inside these institutions was scarcely, if at all better, even late in the eighteenth century and in the early part of the nineteenth. An English practitioner, for many years visiting physician to one of the oldest hospitals, testified before the Committee of the House of Commons in 1815, "Patients are ordered to be bled about the latter end of May, according to the weather; and after they have been bled, they take vomits once a week for a certain number of weeks; after that we purge the patients. That has been the practice invariably for years long before my time; it was handed down to me by my father, and I do not know any better practice." In the institution to whose inmates these enlightened gentlemen prescribed, there were five "keepers," three male and two female, for a hundred and twenty-two patients. The kindly efforts of the physician were supplemented by the liberal use of manacles and chains. The violent were chained about the legs, the arms, the wrists; chained to the floor, the bed, or the wall.

One has well said, "It is difficult to understand why and how they continued to live; why their caretakers did not, except in the case of profitable patients, kill them outright; and why, failing this — which would have been a kindness compared with the prolonged torture to which they were subjected — death did not come sooner to their relief."

<hr>

CHAPTER VI.

THE BEGINNINGS OF REFORM AND IMPROVEMENT.

Humanity changes for the better slowly, and usually under some sort of compulsion. The compulsion may be from within, the power of ideas; or it may be from without, the rougher stimulus of muscular force and violence. Customs and habits are ruts, out of which institutions, societies, communities, and governments have to be pulled or lifted. The process is generally unpleasant, often painful, sometimes apparently destructive. Some objects, old and venerated, are sure to be broken in pieces and trodden into the mire; some things of real beauty and utility, on account of their relations and surroundings, are ruthlessly destroyed. Men who have wrought well, according to their conceptions of truth and duty, are rudely thrust aside or visited with unmerited abuse and insult. Many interests suffer for a while, and society is unsettled and disturbed. The new paths are untrodden, and the surface is uneven. Unexpected obstacles are encountered; mistakes and blunders are made. The new leaders, with the best of intentions, are frequently more abundantly endowed with zeal than wisdom. Conservatism naturally laments, protests, and predicts all manner of direful consequences. Even hopeful and sympathizing men, of timid and fearful temperament, are overburdened with doubts and anxieties.

All these and other conditions hedged up and obstructed proposed reforms and improvements in the treatment of the insane. It required confidence and courage, bordering on rashness and presumption, to take the first steps. It would, however, be a gross libel upon human nature to suppose that humane and Christian men and women were, or could be, satisfied with things as they existed. The apathy of the great body of the people is explained by the fact that very few knew how bad matters really were. The insane could not speak for themselves, and nobody had yet come forward to speak and act for them. Somebody must be found who dared to begin, and who had patience "to labor and to wait." Success, even in a most righteous cause, is not secured in a moment, nor without a struggle. It took years to rouse the public mind to a comprehension of the horrors and barbarism of the slave-trade; it took other long years to break down the iron doors of the filthy dungeons in which "prisoners for debt" were hopelessly immured. The task of cleaning out the reeking cells in which many of the insane were confined, of breaking off their fetters and chains, of bringing them out into the pure air and bright sunlight, and securing for them rational and scientific treatment, was not to be accomplished in a day, nor by weak and intermittent efforts. Old prejudices were exceedingly strong, and medieval ideas about insanity still lingered in many places, both low and high. Slaves were men; debtors were fellow-citizens; but the insane were not even yet quite free from the suspicion of evil associations. They were, undoubtedly, unfortunate and miserable; possibly they might also be wicked and blameworthy. Such feelings were rather felt than expressed; but none the less they influenced conduct and conclusions.

The honor of instituting and leading in reform and improvement belongs to Pinel in France and to Tuke in England. Each of these men labored, for some time, apparently with little or no knowledge of the purposes and efforts of the other. They wrought with different means and under widely different conditions; but both are entitled to much credit and to grateful remembrance. The blessings of many ready to perish have rested upon them and upon their associates and co-laborers.

Pinel was a thoroughly educated physician, and, after having had an experience of a few years in a private institution for the insane, was put in charge of the Bicêtre in Paris, in the year 1792. This establishment was at the same time a prison, almshouse, nursery, hospital, and asylum for the insane. The various classes of inmates were mingled together in the greatest confusion, although the more violent maniacs were confined in a separate quarter of the buildings. Cruelty had rendered these so furious that few persons ventured to approach them, and no one dreamed of freeing them from their chains.

The following extract will show the character of the work which Pinel undertook, and its results. Having obtained permission of the proper authorities, he proposed to try the experiment of liberating some of those who had been longest in confinement. Accompanied by a friend he entered the door of the "great Bedlam of France."

"They were received by a confused noise, the yells and angry vociferations of three hundred maniacs mixing their sounds with the echo of clanking chains and fetters through the dark and dreary vaults of the prison. Couthon, his attendant, turned away with horror, but permitted the physician to incur the risk of his undertaking. He began by unchaining twelve persons. The first was an English officer who had been bound in his dungeon forty years, and whose history everybody had forgotten. His keepers approached him with dread; he had killed one of his comrades by a blow with his manacles. Pinel entered his cell unattended, and told him he should be at liberty to walk at large, on condition of his promising to put on the camisole or strait waistcoat. The maniac disbelieved him, but obeyed his directions mechanically. The chains of the miserable prisoner were removed, the door of his cell was left open. Many times he was seen to raise himself and fall backward,—his limbs gave way; they had been fettered during forty years. At length he was able to stand and to walk to the door of his dark cell. He gazed with exclamations of wonder and delight on the beautiful sky. He spent the day in walking to and fro, was no more confined, and during the remaining two years he spent at Bicêtre assisted in the management of the house.

"The next man liberated was a soldier of the French Guard, who had been in chains ten years, and was an object of general terror. His disorders had been kept up by cruelty and bad treatment. When liberated, he assisted Pinel in breaking the chains of his fellow-prisoners; he became kind and attentive immediately, and was ever after the devoted friend of his deliverer. In a few days Pinel liberated fifty-three. The result was beyond all hope. Tranquillity and harmony succeeded to tumult and disorder; even the most furious maniacs became tractable."

Subsequently Pinel took charge of the Salpêtrière, a similar place of confinement for females, into which he introduced the same humane principles and spirit of reform. The improvement in the condition and treatment of the insane in France commenced with the beginning of Pinel's labors in Paris. He was ably seconded in his efforts by Esquirol, who became his assistant in the Salpêtrière. This gentleman founded an asylum for the insane in 1799, which served as a model for all similar institutions afterwards established in France. Without doubt the great experiment of Pinel had its origin in the feelings and impulses of a generous humanity, more than in the conclusions of scientific medical knowledge, although subsequent investigations and discoveries have proved that his methods were in harmony with the true principles of the science of medicine as well as of the science of mind. In the hands of wise men science, in all departments of human activity, is the handmaid and servant of humanity.

To William Tuke of York, a member of the Society of Friends, belongs the high honor of establishing the

first asylum for the insane in England in which humane
and rational methods of treatment were regularly and
systematically employed. He commenced his efforts in
1792, the same year which saw the beginnings of Pinel's
public labors in Paris. The institution was opened for
the reception of patients four years later. The happy
suggestion of a woman gave to the hospital the name
of Retreat, "to convey the idea of what such an institution should be, namely, a place in which the unhappy
might obtain a refuge, a quiet haven in which the
shattered bark might find the means of reparation or of
safety." It was located on' elevated ground in the
neighborhood of York. The edifice was surrounded by
a garden, and sufficient land was secured for a farm.
The prospect was pleasant and extensive, and pure air
and excellent water were abundant. The building was
unpretentious, like its founder and like the society to
which he belonged. For several years Mr. Tuke per-
sonally superintended the affairs of the Retreat, and
continued to visit it frequently till his death at an
advanced age.

Like most departures from the established order of
things, this pioneer reform asylum encountered some
bitter opposition, and met with serious obstacles and
difficulties. Fortunately, its founder possessed the
somewhat rare combination of a determined, iron will
closely united with a kind heart. His sympathy had
been thoroughly excited, and his sensibilities both
shocked and quickened, by a visit to a hospital in

which he found inmates lying "on straw and in chains." He had, moreover, that peculiar constitution of mind which impelled him to believe that whatever ought to be and needed to be done, could be accomplished by perseverance and hard work.

The nature and extent of the reforms in the treatment of the insane begun at the York Retreat can not be fully appreciated by persons familiar only with the appliances and methods of well-conducted modern asylums. The management of Mr. Tuke and his associates must be contrasted, by means of examples and illustrations, with the prevailing modes of that day. It is, however, profoundly humiliating to be obliged to confess that, after the lapse of nearly a century, contrasts almost as striking can be found between the treatment endured in local receptacles, county houses, and jails, and that employed in our best asylums. The statement of a gentleman who visited at that period a large number of British asylums, for the purpose of examining plans of construction, will be sufficient to indicate, in a general way, the changes and improvements made in the Retreat. He says:

"In some asylums which I have visited, chains were affixed to every table and to every bedpost; in others they are not to be found within the walls. At the Retreat they sometimes have patients brought to them frantic and in irons, whom they at once release and by mild arguments and gentle arts reduce almost immediately to obedience and orderly behavior. A great deal of delicacy appears in the attention paid to the smaller feelings of patients. The iron bars which guarded the windows have been avoided, and neat iron sashes, having all the appearance of wooden ones, have been substituted in their places; and when I visited them, the managers were occupied in contriving how to get rid of the bolts with which the patients were shut up at night, on account of their harsh, ungrateful sound, and of their communicating to the asylum somewhat of the air and character of a prison. The effects of such attention, both on the happiness of the patients and the discipline of the institution, are more important than may at first view be imagined. Attachment to the place and to the managers, and an air of comfort and contentment, rarely exhibited within the precincts of such establishments, are consequences easily discovered in the general demeanor of the patients. It is a government of humanity and of consummate skill, and requires no aid from the arm of violence and the exertions of brutal force."

Under this treatment a man who had been kept chained and naked for twenty years, soon came to wear clothes and to be orderly in his habits and conduct. The change in many others was as marked and as happy.

In addition to the points already mentioned, efforts were made to provide constant employment for those inmates who were able to work. The convalescents were employed as assistants in the care of others; knitting, sewing, and other domestic labors were assigned to female patients; and the men were occupied with such industries as would be most agreeable, as far as means and circumstances would allow.

This experiment at York and a "Description of the Retreat," published by Samuel Tuke in 1813, aroused much public interest in England, and excited some vigorous and angry discussions. Periodicals and newspapers entered into the details. The House of Commons appointed committees and commissions to inquire into the condition of asylums and hospitals for the insane. Acts of Parliament were passed; new institutions were established, and old ones were forced to recognize the progress of the age and the claims of humanity.

Reform and improvement were thoroughly inaugurated, and the condition of the insane began to be rendered more tolerable. Great advances have since been made, but it is not to be supposed that the end has even yet been reached. Progress is still possible.

At the time when Pinel and Tuke commenced their reformatory labors in Europe, only a single asylum existed in the United States devoted exclusively to the insane. A few insane patients were admitted into two or three general hospitals. Of these two or three, the Pennsylvania Hospital was the most prominent and important. As has been elsewhere remarked, it is claimed that the improved and humane methods of the reformers were employed in this institution from the very first. The probabilities are that the claim is well founded. Reform in our own country was needed, not so much in correcting the bad management of existing institutions as in creating a public sentiment which should demand the erection, at public expense, of a sufficient number of asylums to receive and properly care for the victims of insanity who were wandering at large, or were cowering in filth and nakedness in jails and in rude out-buildings, in receptacles of all kinds. The abuse and neglect of the insane among us have never been, to any considerable extent, within the hospitals. Rare and infrequent instances have occurred in these institutions, without doubt; but such cases bear no comparison to those which have taken place, almost daily, in almshouses and other places of detention, and, with shame it must be said, in the seclusion of private and domestic life.

CHAPTER VII.

THE MODERN ASYLUM.

Of any specific form and arrangement of buildings for an asylum I shall not presume to speak. Only a specialist of intelligence and experience can determine, with any authority, matters of that kind. My remarks will have reference merely to such things as an interested observer, under favorable conditions, can readily discover and appreciate.

First of all, it will be universally conceded that the location of an institution for the insane should be healthful and pleasant. The grounds should be ample in extent and, if possible, varied in character. The wearisome monotony of a dead level of surface or of entire sameness of scenery should be avoided. An abundant supply of pure water must be near at hand, and the facilities for drainage and for the removal of

all filth must be excellent. The site should be sufficiently retired to secure freedom from noise and confusion and from undue observation. At the same time
it should be easy of access, both for the convenience of
patients and their friends, and also for the ready trans-
portation of material and supplies. A farm of two or
three hundred acres of rolling land, with a fertile soil,.
not too clayey, with a fair proportion of groves and
woodland, just on the outskirts of some city or village
of considerable size, will best satisfy the requirements
as to location.

The buildings should be, of course, substantial and
durable in character, but the style of architecture
should be light and tasteful. Care should be taken to
avoid all prison-like appearance. Excessive ornamentation adds nothing in respect of beauty, and is incon-
gruous as a matter of good taste. Local pride takes
an unfortunate direction when it demands unnecessary
expenditure upon the external means and appliances
of public charity and benevolence.

The interior arrangements ought to provide, in the
best possible manner, for the care, comfort, and safety
of the inmates. Danger from fire should be especially
guarded against. The horror of a burning asylum for
the insane can be equaled only by that of a burning
receptacle of helpless orphan children. Humanity
shudders at the sight, or even the thought, of either.
Buildings of many stories in height, with narrow doors

and steep and winding stairways, are unsuitable for asylums and hospitals.

Judicious classification of patients is one of the imperative necessities for the proper treatment of mental disease. This must be fully provided for, or the main purpose for which asylums exist will be defeated. On many accounts, the gathering of large numbers of the insane in one institution is not desirable. The possibility of more complete classification, however, is increased by this arrangement; and the advantages derived from the separation of those whose peculiar mental condition renders them unfit associates, will probably offset many real disadvantages. The absolute impossibility of making any tolerable classification of their inmates is a fatal objection to county and other small receptacles, into which all forms of mental disorder are crowded promiscuously together.

An experienced Medical Superintendent says, "Every asylum should have separate accommodations for the following classes of patients: 1. Those convalescing from various forms of mental disease. 2. Those suffering from mild excitement. 3. Those suffering from acute excitement. 4. Those suffering from epilepsy and the advanced stages of paresis. 5. Those suffering from chronic mania. 6. Those suffering from melancholia and states of depression. 7. Those suffering from senile and other quiet forms of dementia. 8. Those suffering from the more active forms of dementia (irritable dementia)."

4

One of the most characteristic features of the modern, improved asylum is this perfect separation of the various classes of patients. The lack of it has been very painfully impressed upon me in visiting several county receptacles for insane paupers. A strong and violent female, gesticulating and shouting under the influence of maniacal excitement, may be seen near by a weak and timid old lady suffering from senile dementia. And in the same apartment may be an epileptic in the midst of a terrible and frightful convulsion. All the better feelings of humanity revolt at the pain inflicted by this promiscuous herding together of the unfortunate and distressed.

In addition to provision for proper classification, the model asylum will have all its rooms, which patients are to occupy, well-lighted, warmed, and ventilated. It ought to be unnecessary to say that no "cells," or apartments of cell-like character, exist in any really modern institution for the insane. Such prison-like arrangements belonged to the age of "chains and fetters," the iron age which preceded the reforms of Pinel and Tuke. If any so-called asylum still tolerates and finds use for them, its managers should speedily give place to others, whose birth and education have been within the present century.

The halls and all the rooms will be made as cheerful as possible by inexpensive ornamentation. If encouraged, many of the inmates will take an active interest in rendering everything as home-like as circumstances will permit. The floors will be painted or oiled, and in some cases carpeted. The walls will be pleasantly tinted, and hung with paintings and pictures. The halls occupied by convalescent and other quiet and orderly patients will be supplied with musical instruments, with papers, periodicals, and books. Conveniences for games and sports will be provided, both within doors and on the grounds. Amusements and recreations of a social character will be frequent, and will be open to all whose condition will allow them to participate, or to enjoy relaxation in this way. Officers, physicians, and attendants all unite to give to a life, which at best must have much of monotony, as much variety and cheerfulness as the circumstances and surroundings will permit.

I am not trying to paint an ideal institution, managed by ideal officers and peopled by an ideal class of inmates. I am only speaking of what I have observed, and of what is practicable in any institution where there is a hearty, earnest purpose to do all that can be done to comfort and to cure.

No asylum or hospital can be made a home in the highest and best sense of that word ; but it can be made to resemble a real home, and to surpass almost infinitely scores and hundreds that are called by that name. If there were more true homes inhabited and animated by the spirit of tenderness, forbearance, and mutual helpfulness, fewer asylums would be required, and the existing ones would be less crowded.

By means of detached cottages and other devices, it will undoubtedly be found possible to add, in many respects, to the home-like character of institutions for the insane, and also of institutions for other classes of the unfortunate and dependent. In public schools for neglected and dependent children, and in reformatories, this is already attempted with a fair degree of success. Beyond certain limits, however, this is not desirable. Life in a public institution, of whatever form and however organized, is not like, and can not be like, real out-of-door, every-day life. To the child or the youth, it is not the best preparation for the actual life into which he must presently enter. The aim should be to keep the child, or the adult even, unless it be for crime, in the institution the shortest possible time. There is less danger of fostering unreal notions of ordinary life in an asylum for the insane than in most other public institutions; but its arrangements should not be such as to create distaste for the kind of life to which the patient must return, or to present too strong temptations for prolonging his residence in the institution. It is due to truth to add that danger in this direction can not become of a serious nature under any conditions at present conceivable.

The modern asylum, I am persuaded, will continue to put forth more and more effort to provide suitable employment for its patients who are able to labor. This will not be attempted for economic reasons. It is not probable that the labor of the insane can be made a source of profit to the institution. For the present, at least, it is more likely to cause an increase of expenditure. Employment will be provided for the same reasons that books and music, amusements and recreations are provided, as a curative agency. Enforced idleness is not merely irksome to men and women in early or middle life and of fair physical health and vigor, who have been accustomed to an active and laborious manner of living, but is a positive source of danger, more especially when the mental balance has been lost. Industrial pursuits of some sort are needed to give an outlet for energy which will otherwise be consumed in acts of destruction and violence, or will find vent in maniacal excitement and disorder. Without doubt, such occupations will enable the managers of asylums to dispense almost entirely with all forms of mechanical or medical restraints. It will be readily conceded that many difficulties must be encountered in providing employment for all classes of the insane. Indeed, I do not conceive it possible to do so with any means now at the command of the officers in charge of existing institutions. I am confident, however, that the near future will see great improvement in this direction.

Some other important characteristics of modern asylums will be touched upon, directly or incidentally, in subsequent chapters.

CHAPTER VIII.

GUARANTIES FOR THE SAFETY AND PROPER CARE OF THE INSANE IN ASYLUMS.

Many of the insane are utterly helpless and defenseless. The infant in the cradle is not more so. Their mental condition is such that they can neither comprehend nor make known to others their wants; and their physical state is such that, if left to themselves, they would soon perish or become repulsive and loathsome. Patients of this class are entirely dependent upon their attendants for cleanliness, for food, and for clothing, while, in not a few cases, they are unable to appreciate kindness or to express gratitude. Even near relatives and personal friends find it not easy to escape the charge of neglect in caring for such pitiable victims of disease.

Other classes of the insane, not so weak in body or mind, are nearly as defenseless and dependent as these. In consequence of the delusions under which they are suffering, or for other obvious reasons, little reliance can be put in what they say. Their stories of the treatment received by them at home are too improbable, and often monstrous, to admit of belief even for a moment. The same inability to distinguish delusions from realities characterizes their statements concerning affairs connected with the asylum. I have myself listened to recitals which, if true, would curdle the blood and kindle hot indignation. It required, however, very little discernment to enable one to see that the things stated could not, by any possibility, have occurred. The result is that suspicion and doubt are thrown over all statements of the insane, and of those who have fallen into any form of mental unsoundness. Consequently reports . of neglect or abuse coming from patients, even though well founded, will have little weight unless corroborated by other testimony. However much to be regretted, this is inevitable. In the great majority of cases no injustice will be done; but occasionally, under these circumstances, a genuine and truthful charge of wrong-doing will be discredited. No candid observer, with ordinary knowledge of human nature, will be disposed to deny this possibility. Where escape from detection is easy, or even seems so, the power of temptation is greatly increased. Experience teaches that bad and heartless men and women, in every relation of life, take advantage of this state of affairs. The family affords illustrations of this as frequently as the asylum or the hospital. The way by which danger from this source can be entirely avoided has not yet been discovered. The practical problem is how to reduce it to the minimum.

Still another fact increases the helplessness and dependence of one class of patients. The probability of restoration from certain forms of mental disease is undoubtedly much greater if the patient can be completely secluded, for a time, from all association with relatives and intimate friends. The chances of recovery may be increased many times over to the wife and mother, by separation for weeks, perhaps for months, from every familiar scene and face, from husband and children and life-long friends. The same may be true of a father and husband, of a son or a daughter. The necessity and advantage of such entire seclusion will naturally be denied by some, and probably questioned by very many. It seems heartless and positively cruel. Observation, however, has left no doubt in my own mind that such a course is sometimes the only one which affords good grounds for hope of ultimate restoration to mental health. The condition is peculiarly sad and trying for the patient and distressing for the friends. It imposes, also, peculiar responsibility upon the officers of an asylum. It is inconceivable that any officer, possessed of the ordinary feelings of humanity, would recommend or advise such separation, unless he deemed it an absolute necessity to successful treatment. Such cases, not unfrequently, open the flood-gates of criticism and abuse. Out of these have grown most of the harrowing tales concerning the horrors of asylum life. It will be freely admitted that patients of this class are, for the time, placed without reserve in the hands of those in charge of the institution. In accepting such trusts, obligations are entered into which a good man would gladly avoid, and which a bad man may violate.

It would be easy to multiply illustrations of the helpless and defenseless condition of a very large proportion of the inmates of any institution for the insane. It would also be easy to show that the condition of the insane outside of asylums is, in a majority of cases, still more helpless and defenseless. This ought always to be kept in mind in considering the subject under discussion. Mental disease, when serious in its character, exposes the sufferer to neglect, or injustice, or abuse, at all times and in all places, in the family, in the community, in the court-room, and in the hospital. Wisdom and humanity demand that all known precautions shall be taken to secure protection and safety.

I have purposely written with plainness. With human nature as it is, there is everywhere danger to the weak and helpless. It were worse than folly to deny its existence in asylums. The question is how to guard against it most effectively. Upon this question I desire to speak with the utmost frankness, because I believe it concerns the well-being of the most unfortunate class of sufferers in human society, and also because I believe the means employed to avert danger often increase it, and the measures adopted to secure safety render the attainment of this next to impossible.

The public mind is justly sensitive in respect to the management of all public institutions. But any institution whose doors can not all be thrown open freely to promiscuous visitation and inspection, about which there is something of reserve and exclusiveness, is in danger of exciting feelings of jealousy and distrust in the ignorant and credulous, and even in those who resent the imputation of ignorance or credulity. Asylums for the insane necessarily belong to this class of institutions. Grant, what is often asserted, that the system of reserve and exclusion has sometimes been carried to an unnecessary extreme; grant that doors have been kept closed which might more wisely have been left open; after all possible admissions, it remains evident to any person of common intelligence that the halls of such an institution can not be exposed unreservedly to the public gaze.

As a result of this necessary exclusion and of other causes, against which no wisdom or prudence can effectually guard, periodical outbursts of popular feeling against asylums and their management are liable to occur. Violent abuse is heaped upon trustees, superintendents, officers, and employees generally. Newspapers are filled with stories of the most fearful and terrible nature. Reports, gathered from all sources, are eagerly received and accepted as reliable evidence of shocking neglects and abuses. Upon such testimony men and women of the noblest character and purest lives are condemned and denounced as monsters of iniquity and cruelty. Legislative and other investigations follow, and elaborate reports are made and published. Some new laws are enacted, and additional provisions are made for visiting and examining boards and commissions.

It would be too much, probably, to affirm that no good results come from such excitements and investigations. But it is beyond question that, in most cases, the evil results greatly outweigh the good. Some bad men may be exposed, removed, and punished. Some abuses may be corrected. But the work of the institution has been thrown into confusion; the inmates have been stirred into feverish excitement; friends of patients have been alarmed and pained; and the community has been filled with false or exaggerated statements, calculated to create a lasting feeling of suspicion and distrust. And, worst of all, the men and women best qualified by nature and acquirements to care for the insane quietly retire, or decline to enter positions where they will be exposed to unmerited detraction and abuse.

It is not by such methods that safety and proper care can be secured for the insane. Various means have been devised, and others have been suggested and zealously advocated. Among such means are laws, and rules and regulations for the organization of asylums, for the admission of patients, and for their proper care, oversight, and discharge. Laws for

these purposes are absolutely necessary, and without
doubt afford some measure of protection to certain
classes of the insane, and particularly to persons who
may, for sinister purposes, be accused of mental
unsoundness. But legislative enactments, however
wisely drawn, can give little guaranty for right treatment of patients within the halls of an institution.
They are not, like the laws of nature, endowed with
a self-enforcing vitality and virtue. To a considerable extent, they must be executed by those whose
conduct they are designed to control and regulate.

Boards of control, commissioners, and visitors are
also accounted among the agencies of safety and protection. Some of these are necessary, and others
may be desirable. There must be some organizing
and managing body, some power to appoint and discharge officers and employees, to exercise oversight,
and to administer generally the financial and other
affairs of an institution. A competent board, intelligent in the direction of its trust, free from partisan
and political influence and dictation, above self-seek-
ing, and not afraid of incurring temporary popular
displeasure, will be a source of confidence to the public, and a guaranty of wise external administration
and of a careful selection of officers to perform the
delicate and varied duties of internal management.
Men of business, practitioners of law and medicine,
students of the science of mind, and practical philanthropists, may well be united in the formation of

such a board. In a general way this body stands between the community and the officers and inmates of the asylum. It is a standing and perpetual "committee of examination and investigation." It should be better able than any other number of persons possibly can be, to protect the innocent and to discover and punish the guilty, if there be any guilty.

Other agencies, supposed to be protective, might be mentioned, but observation has led me to consider them of little real worth. There is, in my judgment, but one guaranty upon which any firm reliance can be placed, and that is *the character and intelligence of the officers in immediate charge of the institution.* Of those officers the Medical Superintendent is the representative and chief. He is the direct executive officer and the responsible head of the asylum. Its spirit and its tone are embodied and incarnated in him. He should have the right to nominate all subordinate officers, and to appoint and dismiss all attendants and other employees. He should be clothed with ample authority, should be allowed abundant room for the exercise of his individual judgment and discretion, and should be held to a corresponding accountability. He should be restricted in his methods of administration by no rules, except such as are clearly necessary. A multitude of petty regulations in respect to the details of internal management, enacted by legislators or governing boards, will often embarrass and hamper a con-

scientious, good man, but are only ropes of sand in
the way of a bad one.   The guaranty of right conduct
must be looked for in the man himself, and not in the
fetters with which he may be shackled.

I am not presumptuous enough to attempt a fin-
ished portrait of an ideal Asylum Superintendent.
It is mere commonplace to say that he should possess
ability, integrity, and intelligence; that he should
have a thorough knowledge of everything which concerns the care and treatment of the insane; and that
he should be well acquainted with all forms of both
healthy and morbid mental activity, and with the
relations of such activity to bodily conditions, so far
as these have been discovered.   It ought to be safe
to assume so much of any person who is permitted to
be a candidate for the Superintendency.   In addition
to all qualifications of this nature, he should be a
thoroughly good man, in the best and highest sense of
the word good—a man into whose hands a husband
would be willing to place the health, life, and honor
of a helpless and defenseless wife or daughter.   He
should be the embodiment of kindness and tenderness, united with great firmness and decision of
character.   His sensibilities should be keen and
quick, while he needs to be free from maudlin senti-
mentality.   It is of the highest importance, also, that
he have power, with no apparent or even conscious
effort, to impress these qualities upon his associates
and employees.   His purpose, spirit, tone, and temper

should pervade, like the unseen essence of peace, love, and mercy, every nook and corner of the institution. Out of him, as out of the greater Physician, should go virtue to heal, calm, and restrain. He should possess that half-divine something which, like a hidden magnet, draws out into spontaneous activity the very best of everything there is in his assistants and subordinates. He thus multiplies himself a hundred-fold, and is constantly, though invisibly, present everywhere in the institution.

In such men, and in the associates and helpers whom they naturally gather about themselves, are found the only sufficient guaranties for the wise and humane treatment of the inmates of an asylum. Without these, all other provisions will have little value; with these, the danger of neglect or abuse is reduced to the lowest possible limit. With the imperfections of human nature, it can never be wholly removed from public institutions or from private homes.

A lady patient of most excellent spirit, a personal friend, writes as follows:

"I understand, as I could not without having been an inmate of such an institution, how entirely a patient is in the power of doctors and attendants. I should be very unwilling to trust myself or my friends to an institution, without knowing the character of its managers. Dr. —— is one of the kindest of men. As one of the ladies, seven years a patient, expressed it, 'He is a father to us all;' and it was a general feeling among the patients that he was their friend and protector. In fact, kindness was one of the essential things in treating patients, as it was very difficult to do anything for them without first gaining their confidence."

This extract, which expresses the feelings of every intelligent patient with whom I ever conversed in respect to the relation of the inmates to the physicians and employees, suggests a few words touching the position and duties of the attendants in an asylum. The importance of their character and duties to the immediate comfort and well-being of patients can not be rightly estimated by any one unacquainted with the interior organization and arrangements of an institution for the insane. They stand nearer to the patients, in many respects, than the physicians. It is in their power to make life to the inmates not only tolerable, but comparatively happy. It is equally within their power to render life anything but tolerable and happy.

A Medical Superintendent says, "Of all the means used in the institution for the comfort and restoration of the inmates, the most important, perhaps, is personal attendance. It alone is applicable to each individual case, and is available by night as well as by day. Upon its character and efficiency, and, more than all else, upon its spirit, the success of treatment in many cases largely depends. With the most complete architectural arrangements, unlimited resources, and skillful medical care, discouraging failure may often attend when remedial effort is applied through harsh, ill-mannered, and ill-tempered attendants. The spirit in which a request for even a drink of water or the adjustment of a pillow is met, may give to a feeble, depressed patient quiet, health, restoring sleep, or, on the other hand, a night of restless irritability."

Another says, " It is undeniable that the efficiency and usefulness of an asylum are largely promoted by a careful, painstaking corps of attendants. From the peculiar nature of mental disease, it is inevitable that patients must be, to a great extent, dependent upon their attendants for companionship, personal care, and direction in occupation and amusement. In sickness the attendant is the assiduous nurse; in convalescence, the faithful and attached friend; and at all times the intimate companion of the patient. It is consequently extremely important that faithful, efficient, self-denying, conscientious attendants be engaged. In selecting them the effort is constantly made to secure the services of persons of unexceptionable habits, and with fitness for the special work. The attendant lives with his patients, eats at the same table from the same fare, occupies rooms similarly furnished and arranged, and is in every sense of the word an attendant.

" The effort is constantly made to develop the family spirit, as it may be termed. Each ward is under the special charge of a person of experience, who for all practical purposes is like the head of a family in the best sense of the word. He is made responsible

5

for the work of the hall and for the comfort and welfare of the patients committed to his care, and is furnished with as much assistance as the work requires."

In the character, habits, and training of these attendants is found a guaranty for the comfort and humane treatment of the insane, scarcely less valuable than that found in the character of the Superintendent and his immediate associates. The lady from whose communication I have already quoted says,—

"In the fall of 1873, finding I was losing control of my mind, and fearing to lose it wholly, I went to the asylum voluntarily. I had all confidence in the institution, from long acquaintance with some of the attendants who had been there for years. I was placed in the convalescent hall, and can speak confidently of that. I received the most careful attention and kindest possible treatment from doctors and attendants; and my case was not exceptional. In this hall were gathered ladies from all the other wards, who had been removed there from time to time, as their condition warranted. As there was no restriction placed upon our social intercourse, I gathered from the general tone of remark by patients and attendants from different halls, that harsh treatment was censured, and that any attendant who was not uniformly kind to the patients was certain of dismissal, if the facts were known at head-quarters."

There is a most unfortunate inclination in the community generally to criticise and censure the attendants employed in an asylum. They are, in some quarters, still spoken of as "keepers," and are pictured as hardened, unfeeling wretches. Nothing could be more unjust than such imputations upon those with whom I have been acquainted. With only very rare exceptions, they have been young men and women of unusual excellency of character, of refined manners, and of good taste. They will rank in culture and intelligence, not with the ordinary domestics of the family, but with the average pupils of our grammar and high schools. Many of them have been teachers, and have exchanged the uncertain position of the school for a more permanent one in the asylum. To secure and retain such attendants, a rate of wages must be paid fully equal to that received by teachers in the common schools. To say nothing of justice to the employees, true economy and the highest interests of the institution unite in demanding such compensation, since good attendants can be secured and retained in no other way.

Many of the duties necessarily required of the employees upon some of the wards of an asylum are of the most taxing and trying nature. The sick are to be cared for night and day. Patients of degrading and uncleanly habits are to be kept in a wholesome condition of body and clothing. Excited and disturbed patients are to be quieted and prevented from doing injury to themselves or to others, and all parts of the hall are to be kept in good order and free from dirt. Some of these duties are so distasteful, not to say repulsive, to the finer feelings and delicate sensibilities of our nature, that even near relatives

and personal friends find it not easy to continue to
perform them for any protracted period. There is
need of a character permeated through and through
with the noblest of principles, and reinforced by all
available motives, if such work is to be done thoroughly and conscientiously, day by day and night by
night, when there is no rational human eye to see,
nor ear to hear, nor tongue to report. That divine
love which " suffereth long and is kind, which bear-
eth all things, endureth all things, and is not easily
provoked," will here find excellent opportunity for
exercise. I am glad to bear witness to the self-re-
straint, zeal, fidelity, patience, and tenderness of many
attendants whom I have known. The outside world
and the casual visitor can never properly estimate
this service.

The securities afforded by the guaranties here
described will be greatly increased by the force of an
enlightened and just public sentiment in the community at large. Under the influence of such a sentiment, there will be a disposition to provide all
necessary means for the protection and care of the
insane, a correct estimate of the value of proper
and timely treatment of those attacked with mental
disease, and a more generous appreciation of the services of physicians and others employed in asylums.
Civilized men are not, unless overcome by passion of
some sort, deliberately and needlessly cruel to their
fellows. Misfortune and suffering touch their pity

and sympathy, and helplessness does not usually appeal in vain for succor and protection. But intelligence is needed, that pity, sympathy, and compassion may be wisely directed.

· Public sentiment has undoubtedly improved within the last few years. More correct notions are entertained of the nature of insanity, of its causes, and of the means by which it may be relieved or cured. Facts, however, compel the humiliating confession that much of ignorance and of old prejudice still survives, and is sometimes found in quarters where we would not expect to meet it. Physicians and clergymen, on account of the peculiar and intimate relations which they sustain to the sick and their families and friends, can do more than persons in other professions and employments to enlighten the people. Next to these, teachers, especially in the higher institutions of learning, have the largest opportunities to do valuable service in this direction. In schools where mental science is taught, attention should be directed to the most obvious causes and peculiarities of morbid mental action, and to the influence of harmful habits, both of mind and body.

CHAPTER IX.

TREATMENT OF THE INSANE OUTSIDE OF ASYLUMS.

As already remarked, the disposition to criticise the interior management of asylums is very general. There is a singular readiness to accept, without questioning, all tales of abuse and neglect, however improbable they may appear. Less eagerness is manifested to learn facts concerning the condition and treatment of the insane in and about our own homes, in the immediate communities and neighborhoods where misfortune has overtaken them. The character of private places of confinement and of public receptacles is not often a subject of examination or complaint. Much unnecessary suffering could easily be prevented, if attention should turn itself, with wise discrimination, to local occurrences and circumstances, and should insist upon the removal or cure of evils within sight and hearing of one's own doors, with the same zeal and earnestness which it manifests for the correction of those at a greater distance. A few cases which have come to my personal knowledge may be safely taken as types of a multitude of others which have found no record. These indicate the existence of a wide field open for cultivation in the interests of humanity and charity, and so near at hand as to be accessible to all.

A soldier from one of the rich counties of my adopted State died of starvation and disease in a prison-pen during the civil war. He left a young widow with two little children in destitute circumstances, in the midst of a well-to-do community. Within a short time the little ones sickened and died, and the widow was alone and childless. She was of unblemished life and reputation, and not altogether uncultivated in mind and tastes. The shock of these repeated sorrows was too much for her weakened body and unstrung nerves. Her mind gave way, and a mild and inoffensive form of insanity came upon her. She heard voices calling her — the voices of her martyred husband and her lost children. She wandered about the neighborhood, and at night went into the grave-yard near by and slept, if sleep came to her relief in her sadness, with her head pillowed upon the new-made graves of her children. The neighbors pitied and sympathized, and did what uninstructed kindness could do. The chill evenings and biting frosts of autumn and early winter came; and one morning she was found helpless and half-dead from exposure to the cold night air. Restored a little, she was sent, in a farmer's wagon, to the county officer whose duties included the care of the poor and unfortunate. When she was brought, he happened to be sitting in a public place with some boon companions. In the most unfeeling manner, he jested on her visits to the "bone-yard," as, in his refined vernacular, he named the resting-place of her lost little children. "Voices call me," she said in weak and piteous tones. "Whose voices? what voices? where do they come from?" said the humane conservator of the public interests. "I can not tell whence they come," she replied in the same sad tones. "Perhaps," said the officer, "they come from Chicago; may be your husband calls you there. Would you like to go and see?" "O, anywhere to find my husband," said she; "O, send me to him." The price of a railroad ticket to Chicago was paid; the impoverished county was freed from the charge of an insane pauper; the faithful public officer chuckled at his economical shrewdness, and the soldier's widow and bereaved mother went alone, friendless and penniless, bereft of hope and reason, to plunge into the seething vortex of a great and wicked city. Language is utterly inadequate to make fitting comment on a case like this.

Another example, less piteous in its termination, illustrates the same tendency to allow considerations of so-called economy to outweigh all regard for humanity. The home of a wife and mother had been wrecked and ruined by a drunken husband. The widow depended upon the labor of her children and her own efforts for her support. Two stalwart sons enlisted in the ranks of the army which saved a nation's life. They died victims of lingering disease and starvation, in the delirium which hunger often produces. A surviving comrade told the harrowing tale to the mother. Its horrors were too much for powers weakened by anxiety and suffering. She became insane. Her disease was not violent in form, but unfitted her to care for herself, and the remaining members of the family were unable to provide suitably for her support and protection. Her residence happened to be on the borders of the Commonwealth. She was consequently tossed across State lines and then over county lines, finding no rest and little pity. At last she was fortunate enough to fall among public officers who did not forget that they were men and were born of mothers, and who did not lay aside humanity when they assumed a little brief official responsibility. Through their efforts she found in an asylum a home, more than earned by the sacrifice of her sons, where proper care will smooth the path down which tottering age goes to its quiet resting-place.

As I am writing, my eye rests upon the following item in a daily paper published in the present year of grace. The circumstances are not within my personal knowledge, but they seem well authenticated.

"There has been found in ———, confined in a filthy pen, in a nude condition, a woman sixty years of age and a lunatic. She owns considerable property. She has been kept in her present condition from the *economy of relatives.*'

It would be easy to multiply instances of a similar and of a more shocking nature. These are sufficient to indicate the need of circumspection which can see things near at hand. A superintendent of the Kalamazoo Asylum, in speaking of some persons received into the institution, says:

"They have sometimes come to us in a condition not pleasant even to describe — often with but few traces of humanity left. To bring these emaciated, broken-down individuals up to their previous standard of physical health, without which improvement is impossible, and to recall habits of personal cleanliness and propriety, is generally a long and tedious process; yet a fair proportion of them have left the institution so much improved as to become again pleasant members of the family circle, and not a few were subsequently able to provide for themselves."

Of the patients received during the first years after the opening of the asylum, he says, "Of the adult females, fully ninety per cent are much broken in health and constitution. Very many are faithful, self-sacrificing wives and mothers, prostrated by toil and anxiety, and maternity met under peculiarly trying circumstances, where the only nursing received is the few hours snatched by kind neighbors from their own duties. In regarding these we can not help but feel a deeper and tenderer sympathy than is enlisted in behalf of those whose sufferings are the result of their own imprudence."

Sometimes, without doubt, such lack of proper care for the wife and mother has been through no fault of the husband and father, or of other friends;

but in too many cases it has been the result of thoughtlessness or of criminal neglect on the part of those who had abundant means to furnish all needed care, and who may justly be held responsible for the suffering which their neglect has caused.

An early report states that, referring to the record of applications for those admitted, it is shown that two had been confined for many months in cages, one of them, as it was expressed, having become like a wild animal. In nine cases homicide had been attempted, though successfully in but one. In reference to two, it was stated that no one could with safety enter the place in which they were confined; in case of twenty-one of the small number admitted, confinement in a jail had been deemed necessary. The devices of restraint and punishment of many presented for admission certainly surpass those depicted by sensational writers. Intentional cruelty is not charged upon those who have had the care of these persons. The bruises, excoriations, and fractures found upon their bodies; the fetters crowding into the flesh; the firmly rusted irons, and the ridges left by the policeman's club, give evidence rather of thoughtless ignorance, or of that strange fear with which the insane are sometimes still regarded."

These things did not occur in the "dark ages" of the far-off past. They are not imaginary fictions conjured up "to point a moral or adorn a tale." They are simple recitals of facts existing about us and among us in the last half of the nineteenth Christian century, in the very bosom of a so-called Christian civilization, only a stone's throw from the school-house and the church.

There is need of guarding, with jealous care, the security and welfare of the inmates of asylums. This is freely conceded. But there is equal, if not greater, need to devise safeguards for the protection and humane treatment of the insane in the jails, receptacles, strong-rooms, cages, and other places where ignorance, fear, or false economy has confined them.

CHAPTER X.

OPINIONS AND FEELINGS OF PATIENTS.

All intimate relationships involve communications of a confidential character. No honorable man, under any ordinary circumstances, will make these known even to personal friends, much less to the public. The physician owes silence to his patients; the clergyman to his parishioners; more than these, the officer of an asylum is bound to seal his lips and his pen to anything the relation of which might bring a blush to the cheek or a pain to the heart. The interior of many a home is thrown open to the superintendent and to others, in an institution whose inmates have been forsaken by judgment and discretion. Skeletons are uncovered whose existence few even suspect. All such revelations are buried and, as far as may be, forgotten. I shall, consequently, speak only of things which belong outside the veil of confidence, but which none the less enable one to understand a little of the experience of the insane themselves.

My observation has left no doubt in my own mind that to some patients the asylum is a place of intense mental suffering. To them it is a "palace-prison" of most irksome restraint and confinement. They almost constantly fret and chafe against necessary rules and regulations. In their own estimation they are not mentally diseased, but are unjustly and wrongly deprived of liberty, either by the machinations of enemies or by the treachery of relations and pretended friends.

These patients have usually a good degree of mental activity, often speak fluently and rationally, excepting upon some particular topic, and write with much vigor and sharpness. The casual visitor will look upon them with great interest, and will be likely, if he does not tarry too long, to question their insanity. In most cases they seem to have inherited a defective physical organization and a predisposition to some form of cerebral disease. Under some unfortunate combination of circumstances their nervous systems have been overtaxed. They have lost self-control, and have fallen under the power of some absorbing delusion. In this condition they become unsafe members of society, frequently a source of danger to their friends, and often incapable of caring properly for self-protection. If educated and ambitious, it is not unusual for them to imagine that some great and peculiar mission has been imposed upon them, to the accomplishment of which life should be sacredly devoted. Of this class more females than males have come to my notice. The extracts given below from letters addressed to me by a young lady will show the intensity of feeling to which patients, suffering under this form of mental impairment, are subject. The lady was a graduate of a literary institution of high rank, and possessed, in certain directions, ability above the average of her associates. My acquaintance with her began before her admission to the asylum.

Sir:—I wish I might stir your heart and the hearts of your coadjutors to justice and humanity. Not to weakly give my confidence that it may be used against me shall I write as I do, but I have depended on you, almost in a frenzy of despair, to liberate me. *Can* you fail me? I can not, *can not* stay. They have hurt me so. It kills me. Only superlatively painful experiences await me here, and to succeed in their schemes for me is as *impossible* to them as it would be to turn the planets from their courses. You can arrange for my friends to come for me and take me to their own tender care, or rather to liberty and long rest from disturbing causes, that systematic labor may once more be possible to me, and the right be mine to live according to the dictates of reason and conscience, and sway the influence a responsible being should, untrammeled by authority and brutality. I believe in myself, and will not yield to the conspiracy against me, though all the world were in the league.   .   .   .

I can not be ruined so. I *must* go. Keep me, if you *dare*. They need not fear what I will say. *They* can say I was insane. But all the imputations of insanity placed on me are false, and with eyes intelligently open I have tried to save my brain. Talent and character were to make my way, and they have tried to rob me of both. . . . Can you imagine anything worse than a heart and brain crushed by all the hellish devices the arch-fiend could prompt, under the regime of a beastly dragon of a woman? In the effort to make me of like passions with themselves they have spared no pains to tear me from my moorings of religion and eradicate all I hold dear. . . . Could you know all of thought, emotion, and purpose that have been born and died within me the past year, you would surely say, this brain-wear were better devoted to practical purposes. It never can be here. Shall any tell of good deeds wrought here by me? No! They thwarted it by their fiendish malignity and brutality. I long for release to care for myself, and do my duty by those who have done so much for me. Those who have done all they could to ruin, need pretend no solicitude for my future. I have none. But I am not the woman to be so trifled with, and will not endure it longer. It is fearful to have them prevent my honest industry, and ruin one of the best brains God ever gave a woman. I must not plead in vain any longer.

Yours, etc.,

Mingled with the entreaties, which came from her very soul, were passages indicating the fearful hold which the fatal delusion had upon her mind. Later, after it was evident to her that hope of liberation through me had failed, she wrote as follows:

SIR: — Because you mocked my *last* hope that you would do what you could in remedying the wrong you did in sending me here, by informing my friends of my desire to be with them, my faith in your character is completely shivered. Two months and a half since, that letter implored your aid, and now I am going to write a letter for you to keep and read to revive your drooping energies and spur your zeal for humanity. . . .

If you can demonstrate that it is wise to come in contact with vice, except to rebuke it; or sickness, except to relieve it; or to live degradingly when one might live nobly, then could you be guiltless in allowing me to remain, But because you have suffered me to languish here, I want you to think of me when you gather around your well-spread table in the society of cultured friends. I want you to see pictures of mad-house revels in the fire-light. I hope the wild winds of winter will shriek in your ears of my misery. When you retire to rest think of maniac shrieks, moans, and coughs I sometimes hear. In your honored position of usefulness, think how I am wasting my time and talents. . . . . The suttee is abolished; the horrors of the Inquisition have ceased; American slavery is dead. Russia owns no serfs; but Michigan has an institution where sane, innocent women may be thrown into a smelting furnace among seething specimens of humanity, to be molded into such shape as ———— thinks proper. Every softened lineament may be stricken from the features; nearly every noble emotion from the soul. Remember all this when thankful men and women come to you and say, "You have saved me, under God." Remember that man may praise and admire you, but God looks on the heart. To him you must answer for this wrong; with him I leave you; as for me I have learned that it is better to trust him "than to put confidence in princes."

Yours, with all *due* respect,

                                        ———— ————

P. S. The subject is inexhaustible. Go your way! Wrap the filthy rags of your righteousness closely about you, and be careful about sending another sane, virtuous woman to be placed in the hands of those who were more respectably occupied in cock-fighting and bull-baiting than in doing violence to all the holiest, best feelings of a woman's nature. . . .

This letter also contained, in the suppressed passages, striking illustration of the strength of her delusion. It is a well-recognized fact that insanity of certain types manifests itself much more fully and clearly in the writing than in the conversation of the patient. I can hardly imagine a situation more torturing to the soul than that of a person afflicted with this form of mental disorder. Trust in humanity and trust in God usually die. Hope gradually fades away, and relief comes, in a majority of cases, only through the decay of mental power which confinement probably hastens. Heart-rending tales like that of the "Palace-prison" have their origin in cases of this kind.

The extracts next following indicate a type of mental aberration which not only does not give pain mentally to the patient, but on the contrary seems to afford an almost unlimited source of enjoyment. The imaginary possession of divine power is a delusion not uncommon, particularly among males.

To THE MEDICAL FRATERNITY THROUGHOUT THE EARTH:

Glory to God in the Highest!!! Peace, good will unto all men that shall obey my royal will and pleasure, from this time henceforth and forever. Amen! Amen!! Amen!!! I am the Alpha and the Omega, the beginning and the end, the first and the last. "I am the vine." I am the fulfillment of God's promise to David, 1st Book of Chronicles, 17 chapter, 11th to and including the 15th verse; Psalms the 2d, 7th verse to the end; Revelation, 19th chapter, 16th verse. I am the Lord thy God, and thou shalt have none other God beside me. My yoke is easy and my burden is light. Love one another.

(Signed) ———— ————,
King of Kings and Lord of Lords.

6

ORDER No. 2.

To E. H. Van Deusen, M. D., Principal; George C. Palmer, M. D., 1st Assistant; E. G. Marshall, M. D., 2d Assistant.

KALAMAZOO, MICHIGAN, INSANE ASYLUM.

MY DEAR SIRS, BROS., COMPS., AND SIR KNIGHTS:—You will instruct all in authority under you, from this time, henceforth and forever, to obey my royal will and pleasure in all things that I may desire or ask for; to open all Doors at my command, furnish all necessary information, and attend in every respect to my royal will and pleasure. For my yoke is easy and my burden is light. Amen! Amen!! Amen!!!

Royal Palace of the King of Kings and Lord of Lords, Kalamazoo, Mich.

(Signed)   ——— ———,

King of Kings and Lord of Lords.

KALAMAZOO INSANE ASYLUM,
FEB. 28, 1874.

Shortly after I was thirty-five, I took up the Lord's Power, or the Power which the Lord Jesus laid down; which gave me full Power, which is the Power of the Lord. And at that time, the 10th of April, 1866, I received a mark on my left side like unto a wound, which was healed, which indicated and signified that the head which was wounded unto death was healed and restored to power.   .   .   .   ——— ———.

SEPT. 17, 1875.

To DR. ———:—I have transmitted evidence to you that a general doom is settling on the human race, unless certain conditions are complied with; if those conditions are not complied with, the doom of the human race will be sealed the last day of next February.

Now, the way to prevent the doom of the human race from settling down is to comply with what is demanded and required. Submit to the burdens which the Lord imposes.   .   .   .

I demand and require of you to force the battle and doom on to the President and Vice-President with sword and saber, and with shot and shell, and horse and rider, and to strike for life. Authority is found in being the Lord.

Written by the Creator of all things.

Truly, ——— ———.

The feelings of many restored patients, toward the asylum and its officers, may be gathered from the tone of the letters which follow. These are samples of letters frequently received by the Superintendent and others connected with the institution. They were addressed to me with no expectation of their publication.

DEAR SIR:—In the hope of seeing and conversing with you again before departing from the asylum, I bade you adieu without expressing the great obligations I am constrained to feel myself under to you, in common with my other kind friends, whose instruction and influence contributed so much to my restoration to health and, what is of almost infinitely greater value, to *reason*. You may be surprised when I tell you that of all the influences brought to bear upon my wandering mind and despairing heart, none were more effective in restoring that mind to a healthy tone, and illumining that heart with the light of hope, than the simple religious exercises conducted by yourself. It had been many months since I had listened to any religious exercises, and the very name of Jesus was like a sweet but long-forgotten strain of music to my ear. I always feel that I should like of all things to converse with you upon the themes so dear to every soul that has once realized its own sinfulness, or sought and hoped for mercy at the feet of a loving Saviour. But whenever you came there seemed to be so many who were really greater sufferers than myself, to claim your sympathy and attention, that I was fain to deny myself the pleasure of seeking words of instruction and encouragement for myself during your very welcome visits. Having lost this very desirable opportunity, I will endeavor to make amends to myself by talking with you a little bit on paper, with your consent, upon subjects of vital importance to me, as they involve my spiritual well-being. I said to you that I hoped that I was a Christian, and I do trust I am not presumptuous in thus hoping, still less in trying to regulate my life by the law of Christ, seeking to bring every thought into captivity to his will. But when I look back upon my past life, when I for a moment turn my eye upon my own heart, I become doubtful, and that heart fails me for fear. My Christian experience (if I have had any genuine religious exercises) has been of a somewhat extraordinary character, in which mere feeling had, I fear, too great a share. You may, however, be better able to judge of this when you know something of my education and training. [Here is given a frank recital of personal history and experience, deeply interesting and touching in its character, but intended, as indeed the whole letter was, only for the eye of a sympathizing friend.]

Excuse my prolix epistle, and be so kind as to answer.

Ever your grateful friend,

———— ————.

My Dear Friend and Brother:—My only apology for this intrusion is that I know it will rejoice your heart to hear from *me* that my reason is perfectly restored, and my physical health is much improved, my confidence in the blessed God more firmly established than ever, and the precious promises of the dear Savior a more perfect rest to my soul. I also thought it would encourage your heart and strengthen your efforts in your labors of love with those poor afflicted ones, with whom I was so long associated, to know that your self-denial has not been in vain. Your weekly visits, prayers, and exhortations were so refreshing to *me*, and seemed to be the blessed means of re-awakening that *light, love, joy*, and peace which I had before enjoyed, and which I still retain. Last Sabbath I received the Holy Sacrament of the Lord's Supper, for the first time in two years. You may be sure it was to me not only a solemn, but also a most delightful season. The elders received me at the sacred altar with tears of sympathy and holy joy. Bless the Lord, O my soul, and forget not all his benefits. . . .

Though I have severe trials that often blind my eyes with tears, they are, thanks to our heavenly Father, all outward, and only serve to increase and confirm the imperishable treasure within. "In the world ye shall have tribulation," is a part of the promise, "but in me ye shall have peace." Dear brother, my heart is full, and I would say much more, but fear I am already trespassing. I would be affectionately remembered to Mrs. Putnam. I always think of the pleasant visits at your house with grateful pleasure.

Yours,   ——— ———.

CHAPTER XI.

SCHOOLS AND INSANITY.

In this and some following chapters I wish, if possible, to direct attention to a few topics of practical importance. It is not anticipated that any new truths will be presented, but only that some familiar ones may be looked at from a different direction.

The schools have been accused of many and grave faults. Like scape-goats, they have been loaded down with a huge burden of "transgressions and sins." It has not, however, been charged that they are directly responsible for any considerable amount of mental disease. It would be rank treason for a teacher to whisper that such a charge could have the shadow of foundation. But a practiced observer will, in many cases, discover the real, original cause of insanity far back of the assigned one, in some native tendency of mind, fed and fostered by unwisdom of parents and teachers. Considerable numbers of both students and teachers are found in the asylums. It would not be strange that I should have had a special interest in studying such cases. I have no hesitation in affirming that the arrangements and methods of work in the schools are pretty directly responsible, in a majority of instances, for the insanity of the teachers whose cases have fallen under my own observation. Other causes, without doubt, have conspired with these, but to those the sad result has been mainly due. To put the matter in the briefest possible form, in many schools the organization and administration are such that some of the teachers, usually ladies, are subjected to overwork and over-anxiety. Unreasonable demands are made upon both the physical and mental powers. As a consequence, the vital energies are prematurely exhausted; the nervous system is broken down; the power of self-control is weakened; depression of spirits follows, and finally melancholia, or some other species of mental disease, supervenes. Recovery, in these cases, is doubtful. The best that can ordinarily be hoped for is partial restoration, and a few subsequent years of painful and enforced inactivity and dependence. It would be easy to recall and describe specific examples by way of illustration, but the sanctity of official obligations and other obvious reasons forbid this.

Many female teachers are required to control and instruct too many pupils, to teach too many subjects, to do too much work outside the school-room in preparing matter for lessons, in looking over and marking "examination papers," in filling up blank reports, and in other kindred labor. They are compelled, by methods of examining, grading. and promoting pupils, to undergo too much, too frequent, and too long-continued anxiety, and they are, in not a few cases, left with too little freedom for the exercise of individuality. The responsibility for these evils rests partly upon teachers themselves, more upon principals and superintendents, and largely upon school-boards and the general public.

Little interest has been manifested in this feature of the school question. It has received no discussion in reports, periodicals, or newspapers. It has seemed, therefore, the more needful to give utterance to a few words of unvarnished truth in this connection. Teachers have claims upon justice and humanity, in common with the children whom they help to fashion into manhood and womanhood.

The effects of school requirements and discipline upon the whole nature, physical, mental, and moral, of pupils have been topics of frequent and free discussion. Viewed from a teacher's position, these discussions have involved much of truth, and not a little of misapprehension; and occasionally they have manifested a lamentable ignorance of facts and

principles.   Schools and teachers and educational
methods are justly chargeable with grave faults, but
they are not the sources of all the ills under which
society suffers.   Some things they do which ought
not to be done; they leave undone more which they
should do.

Education of the right sort, the harmonious development and training of the whole complex being of
the child, should conduce to mental health and vigor,
and should do much to prevent insanity.   Schools
are not hospitals or asylums, and it is not their province to reform criminals, to cure bodily diseases, or
to heal mental maladies.   But it is a part of their
legitimate business to prevent all these.   They are
very near the fountain out of which character and
conduct flow.   They should help to guard this from
pollution.   The stream of young life ought not to be
poisoned at its source.   In the interests of mental
health a few things may be demanded, with a good
deal of emphasis, of the home and school, of parents
and teachers.   Some of these are so obvious that
their mention may excite surprise.

(1) Children should be taught, beginning in the
home, obedience and respect for authority.   The
general interests of society demand this; but it is not
urged here for that reason.   A child who frets and
fumes at every command which crosses his inclinations, at every requirement for which he can not
comprehend the purpose, is in a state of constant

nervous irritation. The organs of the body most closely related to mental life can not perform their functions properly. The condition of mind corresponds to the condition of body. Neither has a normal and healthy growth. The habit of rebellion becomes chronic. The child resists the authority of home and the school, and later of society and the state. He is in a condition of perpetual warfare. There is no quiet rest of nerve or brain, and no steady action of the intellect or moral nature.

Let such a person be attacked by some acute disease, the proper treatment of which requires perfect rest of body and mind, and complete submission to the directions of a physician; and the chances of recovery are seriously lessened by his character and habits. There can be no question that a mind permitted to grow up in this way is more liable to insanity, and has fewer chances of recovery.

(2) Children should be taught self-control. Self-control is more than simple mastery over one's temper. That is of prime importance, but it is only the first step. That must be acquired, if the child is to have a well-balanced mental organization. There must be also control of appetites, both natural and acquired; control of all the passions; control of every feeling; control of the mental powers; in a word, of the whole being. One of the highest ends of education, so far as the individual himself is concerned, is to bring every power and faculty into

perfect submission to the will. Then self-control is fully attained. To all children, but especially to those of nervous and highly sensitive organizations, the proper mastership over the sensibilities is of vital importance. If there should be a tendency in the nature to give way to morbid feelings, to "brood" over things, to be moody and capricious and irritable without apparent cause, the greatest possible care should be taken to counteract this tendency by wise methods. With such an inheritance, the beginnings of positive mental disease will be very easily made. Right instruction and training in this respect by parents and teachers, would have saved many of the inmates of our asylums from a fate worse than death.

(3) Moral instruction and training should be given. These must begin in the home, where the life of the child begins. The school must second and carry forward the work of the home. Right impulse must be given; the seeds of right habits must be planted; sound principles must be inculcated. Feelings of duty and obligation must be excited, moral judgment instructed, and conscience quickened. The connection between the moral and intellectual natures is so intimate that disease in one can hardly fail to be communicated to the other. It is doubtful if moral corruption, in certain directions, can co-exist with perfect mental health. Certain it is that some forms of moral pollution and degradation are precursors or attendants of some forms of mental disease.

(4) Instruction should be given in respect to the nature and effects of alcohol, tobacco, and other narcotics, both in the home and in all institutions of learning where pupils are old enough to be profited by it. The relation of these articles to insanity has been discussed elsewhere.

(5) In institutions of higher learning instruction should be given in respect to the action of mind, both in health and in disease, in respect to the relation of body and mind, and the influence of the one over the other. The importance and power of inherited tendencies should be so explained and illustrated as to produce, if possible, a practical effect upon conduct, not only during student-life, but subsequently in a business or professional career, and in the formation of the most intimate domestic relations.

(6) Artificial incitements to study, such as prizes, etc., should very seldom, if ever, be employed. I am not unaware that excellent men and successful instructors hold different views. None the less, however, I have a deeply rooted conviction that such means of stimulating the activity of students are open to the most serious objections, both upon moral and mental grounds. The moral objections are not in place here. Their natural influence upon the intellect is the primary consideration, and, as necessarily related to this, their effect upon the bodily health and vigor. Referring to this subject, a writer says,—

"Let me tell you what I have seen in Christian New England. Two brilliant, high-hearted youths, the rival leaders of their class, all the rest left behind, stretching across the four-years' course neck and neck, stimulated by the spirit of an eager emulation, sacrificing health and peace, only to drop, one into a grave and the other into mental perversion, at the end of the heat."

This is an extreme case, but hardly less sad ones can be found in every asylum. I have in mind examples of hopeless imbecility, resulting from unwise stimulation of faculties precociously developed, and consequently immature and unable to endure the strain of steady and continued effort. In almost all such cases the mental, and often the physical, organization is defective and unstable. Less, and not more, than the usual amount of intellectual labor should be imposed upon children of this sort. Out-of-door sports, and not in-door reading and study, should be prescribed and encouraged.

In primary and secondary schools any system of examinations and markings which causes constant anxiety and strong nervous excitement, on the part of pupils of average abilities and attainments, is to be condemned, and ought to be forthwith abolished. Possibly "average standings" may be lower, though this is not certain; but the average health, tone, and spirits of scholars will be vastly higher.

The physical and mental health of both pupils and teachers will be kept in better condition, and more work of real value will be accomplished, if school arrangements, methods, and lessons are such that the school-room, with its perplexities and tasks, can be wholly forgotten during twelve out of every twenty-four hours.

It is unnecessary to say that I have little sympathy with the indiscriminate abuse heaped upon schools and teachers by some writers whose knowledge of the actual requirements and interior workings of schools is derived from hasty casual visits, or from the statements of over-ambitious scholars returning home with "armfuls of books and bundles of papers" covered with historical questions and mathematical problems, or from the stories of parents whose children are suffering from evening parties, and late hours, and unwholesome diet, more than from school tasks and regulations. I am speaking from the inside, from the teacher's desk, and from abundant means of observation. With rare exceptions, it is not overwork by which children are harmed. The evils result from the unfavorable conditions under which the work is done — conditions which violate the laws of mental hygiene as well as of common sense. The friction of an ill-fitting harness exhausts the draught-horse more than a heavy load. The necessity of keeping step with those whose gait is altogether unlike our own tires more than the walking. Intellectual gaits differ as widely as physical ones.

By some means the lower schools must afford more room for individuality, both in teachers and scholars; personal mental peculiarities should receive more study and attention; less value should be attached to the results of stated or occasional examinations, and more to the character of daily work. "The acquisition of mental power is more to be desired than the acquisition of knowledge. The power to do is worth more than the power to tell what others have done. The ability to comprehend and apply principles outranks, in practical importance, the ability to remember facts and repeat them in chronological order."

<hr />

CHAPTER XII.

RELIGION AND INSANITY.

Among the assigned causes of insanity in asylum reports "religious excitement" appears. Cases of mental disorder classed under this head usually have their recognized beginnings in close connection with those seasons of special religious interest and activity called "revivals." A peculiar sensitiveness in regard to cases of this kind exists in some quarters. A disposition is manifested occasionally to deny, or at least to doubt, the correctness of the classification. It seems to be supposed that, in some way, the imputation of insanity to this cause casts reproach upon religion. There is also, on the part of those who reject certain doctrines and disapprove certain methods, an inclination to over-estimate the number of cases thus produced, and to exaggerate the evils springing from methods which they condemn. They who deny too much and they who affirm too much are, so far as observation enables me to judge, about equally in fault. The cause of truth is never harmed by a frank admission of well-established facts, nor benefited by the assumption as authentic of that which, at best, is only possible or probable.

It is undeniable that attacks of violent insanity can be directly traced to so-called "religious excitement." It is equally certain that such cases are infrequent. Out of one thousand and twenty patients admitted to an asylum, eighteen cases were attributed to this as the probable exciting cause. In some institutions the percentage will be greater, in others less. It is only an act of justice to add that tables of assigned and probable causes are usually very unsatisfactory to those who prepare them. Comparatively few attacks of insanity are due to a single definite cause. More frequently the disease is produced by a combination of conditions and circumstances, no one of which alone would have brought about the result. Some of the causes may have been in operation, entirely unsuspected, for a long time. The assigned cause may be merely the accidental occasion of the final outbreak. This is, without doubt, true of a considerable proportion of the victims of so-called religious insanity.

A few statistics of a somewhat general character may be of interest. Up to the time when four hun-

dred and seventy-three patients had been received into
the Michigan Asylum, just about one-half were members of some religious organization. Of these seventy-
one were Methodists, forty were Roman Catholics,
thirty-three were Presbyterians, twenty-three were
Baptists, twenty-one were Episcopalians, nineteen
were Congregationalists, six were Friends (Quakers), •
five were Universalists, and the remainder were
divided, by ones and twos, among various other
denominations. As would naturally be expected, a
much larger proportion of females than of males were
communicants of churches. My impression is, also,
that forms of insanity which would be called religious
are relatively more frequent among women than
among men. This would be anticipated when it is
remembered that the emotional element is stronger in
the female mind, as a rule, than in the male.

Both the records of asylums and personal observation will justify the general conclusion, I believe,
that no one recognized form of religious faith can be
specially charged with the production of insanity.
It does not appear that the members of one church
are more liable to attacks of mental aberration than
members of any other. Nor does it appear that the
peculiar doctrines of an accepted creed exert an
appreciable influence upon the character of mental
delusions.

It is due, however, to truth to say that individuals
of peculiarly nervous and unstable organizations can

not safely be exposed to long-continued excitement of any sort. The danger will be still greater if such an unfortunate organization has been inherited. Exhaustion from over-work, from disease, from loss of sleep, from anxiety, or from any other cause, brings many persons into a most critical condition. Under such circumstances, any intense excitement may destroy the mental equilibrium and fatally weaken the power of self-control. Undoubtedly religious truths are calculated to stir the sensibilities more profoundly than any others. These truths may be, and sometimes are, so presented as to appeal to the emotions and the imagination more than to the judgment and reason. The resulting state, of both body and mind, is one of peculiar danger to persons of delicate health and of highly nervous temperament, especially if exhausted by labor and harassed with cares and anxieties. In some cases, without question, insanity follows — insanity which might probably have been avoided, if all parties concerned had possessed more knowledge and exercised more judgment and prudence. Some such cases, though not a large number, have fallen under my own observation.

The spiritual nature is so closely allied, at all points, with the intellectual, and both these are so intimately associated with the physical organization, that those who are dealing with one need to understand something, at least, of the laws which govern the others, of the mutual relations between them, and

7

of the influence exerted by each over the others. Without such knowledge the religious character and condition of many persons can not be justly estimated, nor can they be wisely advised and guided. It is clearly the duty of pastors and other religious teachers and guides to become acquainted with the whole complex nature of man, and to study also the individual characteristics of the members of their churches and congregations. It is a deed of greater kindness to save one from disease than to heal him after he has been attacked. Limits must sometimes be put to the religious exercises and labors of individuals of peculiarly impressible and excitable organizations. They are exposed to the danger of being "religious overmuch" in certain directions, a danger from which men in general are entirely free. Such persons, under the reaction which is sure to follow too protracted and exhaustive labors, even for the best of objects, easily fall into a state of mental depression. This assumes the form of spiritual depression and darkness. Light, joy, and peace are gone. They imagine themselves the greatest of sinners. For them there is no hope; they are beyond the reach of mercy or love. They may be of the purest religious character and of spotless lives, may have abounded in practical good works; — all this serves to increase, rather than to diminish, the crushing load which weighs them down. They affirm, with the utmost sincerity, that their whole past lives have been hollow, meaningless shams; that they have never known true religion, or, if they have, are now fallen below the possibility of recovery. Only the "blackness of darkness" is in reserve for them.

Now, first of all, in dealing with such cases, the wise friend and guide will enter into no arguments or reasonings. The border line between sanity and insanity has been crossed. These present manifestations are not causes, but consequences, of disease. The remaining hope is that the delusion, whose hold may not yet be very firmly fixed, can be shaken off. Arguments, by keeping the attention of the patient directed toward the false notion, will only serve to fasten it more deeply and thoroughly in the mind. The current of thought must be changed, and set running in some other direction. Worldly employments will be better than spiritual ones for this purpose. Almost any other conversation will be more wholesome than religious exhortations or consolations in this morbid condition. Fitting amusements and recreations will be more salutary than fastings, and prayers, and self-examinations.

The following extract, from a long letter written to me by a restored patient, will illustrate the danger of which I have spoken. After describing some conditions and exercises to which she had been subjected for a considerable time, she says:

"But this state of things did not long continue. One morning there suddenly fell upon me a trembling consciousness of sin, and an indefinable fear took possession of me. But as I stoutly resisted what seemed to me a weak and unworthy feeling, it soon passed away, to return in a few hours with an array of terrors that could not be allayed. Suddenly as the lightning illuminates the sky, it seemed to me that the very heavens were opened, and I *saw* the awful majesty of God. Involuntarily I closed my eyes, as if to shut out the terrible brightness of the vision. For one single moment my whole soul was drawn upward in aspirations towards that unapproachable holiness, but the next, the fearful conviction that it could never be, that I was not only a sinner, but the very chief of sinners, rushed upon me with such crushing weight that I should have been helplessly stricken to the earth, but for the supporting arms of those about me. I gave expression to my mental agony, and was pointed by a single Christian friend to the Saviour, when I found, to my horror, that I did not and never had believed in his ability to save.

"My great sufferings threw me quickly into a brain fever, from which I only slowly recovered after weeks of the most painful sickness, and such mental and spiritual conflict as I pray God I may never know again. For many long months I found no spiritual peace. I felt myself abandoned of God and man, secluded myself from society, and gave myself up to remorse and despair. In vain I prayed; in vain I wept tears of bitterness; in vain I listened to exhortations and prayers. I actually believed that God's infinite power could never save me, his mercy never reach me. I reasoned that God could never love me because I was a sinner, and it was his nature to hate what was sinful and unholy. It is not my purpose to recapitulate all the conflicts through which I passed, the long and painful process of reasoning and reading through which I at last became convinced of the possibility of an atonement; for, spite of my education, I now saw an atonement to be absolutely requisite even for the purest saint, much more for such a rebel as I felt myself to be. But I did believe it at length, intellectually at least; but yet I had gained nothing, for this Saviour, loving and all-sufficient as he was, could avail *me* nothing. I was all sinfulness, and he must everlastingly hate me.

"But there came a change, and for many weeks my heart was literally burdened with a sense of Christ's love, though I still felt he could never save me from sin and misery. I felt he had waited all my life long to be gracious, and was finally forced to yield to the overwhelming consciousness that, despite my wicked heart, he could make me loving and submissive; and, in all humility, I gratefully accepted the cup of salvation from his bountiful hand.

"But my periods of enjoyment were comparatively brief, though intensely rapturous, so much so as to make me fear that they were merely the excitement of highly wrought feelings. While they continued I could not doubt their genuineness, but when they passed away I grew doubtful and rebellious. After more than a year of such intense suffering, relieved only by brief intervals of spiritual exaltation, I was again attacked with brain fever, during which I lay at the point of death for many days, being constantly delirious, and was left in a state of confirmed insanity which was not relieved until after I came to the Asylum."

It is more than probable that all this intense suffering and many long months of almost hopeless insanity might have been prevented, if parents and teachers and spiritual guides had understood better the laws of physical and mental and religious life.

A singular phenomenon presents itself in some cases of mental disease. The delusion under which a patient labors is of a religious or a semi-religious character, although the previous life has not been in any respect, not even by profession, religious; nor has the mind of the person, so far as can be ascertained, ever been specially inclined to dwell upon religious subjects. I recall a stout and somewhat florid gentleman, whose life, as I understood, had not been remarkable for piety or regularity, who often insisted on removing his garments so as to allow me to examine the scar remaining from the wound inflicted by the spear of the Roman soldier. At one time two gentlemen, each of whom believed himself to be possessed of supreme power, were associated upon the same ward of the asylum. Neither of these patients, as appeared by the history of their cases, had been distinguished for reverence and regard for the Deity. One unacquainted with the vagaries of the insane would naturally conclude that delusions of this sort must have their origin in religious causes. No conclusion could be farther from the truth. The notions upon which the mind fastens in its unbalanced condition seem to have as little relation to the ideas of the previous sane state as dreams have to the every-day occurrences of waking life. Some occult law may act in both cases, but no such law has yet been discovered.

Not unfrequently the moral nature appears to be completely changed by an attack of mental disease. Persons, even ladies, who have been above all reproach, pure in deed and word and thought, become offensive in conduct, and profane and vulgar in speech. Modesty, piety, and good taste seem to have been wiped out of the soul for the time. Though deeply and profoundly religious when in health,

every vestige of religious faith and character van-
ishes. No connection, so far as I know, can be
traced between these abnormal manifestations and
the causes of insanity. As in the cases previously
mentioned, the insane condition furnishes but little
indication of the original disposition, temper, training,
or habits. It would be quite possible for "religious
excitement" or intellectual over-work to be followed
by mental disorder of a gross and repulsive form.
Such facts have to be borne in remembrance when
considering cases of so-called religious insanity.

Leaving aside peculiar and exceptional cases, I am
confident that an intelligent religious faith tends to
preserve mental health, and, when this health has
been impaired, helps the process of restoration. A
firm belief in a wise and just and good over-ruling
Power, who can be trusted and loved, even though
his ways are sometimes "past finding out," gives to
the weakened and trembling mind a much-needed
resting-place. A consciousness of the presence and
personal friendship of this Divine Being supplies a
haven of refuge when alarms, confusions, and anxieties come in to annoy and disturb. The testimony of
not a few restored patients has served to confirm my
confidence in the healing power of true religion.

CHAPTER XIII.

ALCOHOL AND INSANITY.

If one were seriously to affirm that he had something new to say of alcohol and its influence upon human society, he would expose himself to the suspicion of laboring under a mental delusion. The subject has been discussed apparently in all its aspects. If any good comes, or can come, from the use of alcohol, it is safe to conclude that somebody has discovered and made it known. The catalogue of evils with which it stands charged is already so long and so fearful that the addition of another to the list would hardly be noticed. I am not so presumptuous as to expect to make such addition, or to darken the shadows in the picture of human woes produced by the use of intoxicating liquors.

The mind is so constituted, however, that some truths have to be impressed upon it, or thoroughly fastened in it, by dint of repetition. This is especially the case when appetite and passion stand opposed to judgment and reason, and when gratification is immediate and evil consequences are remote and partially hidden. Besides, new members of society are constantly taking their places upon the stage of human activity, and children do not inherit the wisdom of their parents. At best they only receive by transmission the capacity and disposition to learn. They must be taught the same lessons which have been already taught over and over again. Just here many most excellent and zealous reformers and other good people fall into a natural but unfortunate fallacy. They declare that certain things "are settled." But the fact is, however much we may regret it, that nothing is ever finally and permanently settled which has its basis in the deductions of reason, or in conclusions drawn from experiment, so long as every man does his own reasoning and makes his own experiments. Things which depend upon instinct, upon intuition, and upon authority, may be settled; but authority must be uniform and absolute, or it goes for nothing.

The war against alcohol and its brood of evils and horrors will consequently have to go on, and be fought over with each successive generation, unless human nature shall meet with some happy transformation. The greed of appetite and the greed of gain are mighty forces, and are alike deaf to the appeals of reason. Men will continue to manufacture and sell, and other men will continue to drink alcohol in various forms, though every draught helps to produce idiocy, insanity, and murder.

Statistics prove, beyond all reasonable doubt, that intemperance is one of the prolific causes of mental disease. Its work, however, is largely indirect, and is not to be estimated by the number of inebriates committed, during any given period, to asylums for the insane. Alcohol poisons the blood and corrupts the very fountain of life. The drunkard transmits to his posterity woes from which premature death may kindly relieve him. Yet the cases of disease caused directly are very numerous. Dr. Tuke, in speaking of insanity among the laboring classes in England, says, "Among the causes, *intemperance unmistakably takes the lead.*" In France the consumption of alcohol doubled from 1849 to 1869. During the same period mental disease increased fifty-nine per cent. among men, and fifty-two per cent. among women. A larger part of this increase could be traced pretty directly to the increased use of alcohol. At the Worcester asylum nineteen per cent. of the admissions were charged to intemperance during four years, when the habit of drinking liquor was very general. During four years when the temperance movement was at its greatest height, only four per cent. were due to this cause.

Dr. Stearns states that more than ten per cent. of 5000 cases in the Hartford Retreat were caused by the use of alcohol, without including cases of inherited tendency produced by the habits of parents. In all asylums cases of the latter sort are much more numerous than those attributed directly to intemperance. If to the cases caused directly and by inheritance we add the cases produced by want, by overwork, by sufferings both of body and mind among the families and friends of drunkards, certainly one fourth, and probably fully one third, of all the insanity in the country must be charged to alcohol. I do not include in this statement cases of idiocy and imbecility, of which it is, without question, the most prolific cause.

If zeal which outruns judgment is ever excusable, or even rises to the rank of a virtue, it is when the question of dealing with the production, sale, and use of intoxicating liquors is under consideration. What to do about the traffic in such liquors, and their use as beverages, is the great problem of our age, and its solution requires all the practical wisdom of statesmen and philanthropists. The question is too broad and deep to be "settled" by narrow partisanship or angry denunciation. Genuine humanity and sound political economy must join in the final solution. Meanwhile a great work of education is to be done for and upon the young in our homes and in the schools. The nature of alcohol and its effects, both upon the drinker and upon his offspring, must be thoroughly taught, as well as the enormous taxation which it inflicts upon society. It will not be sufficient simply to give instruction. Knowledge is not all, or even the most, that is needed. The moral nature of the growing citizen must be reached and enlightened. A feeling of responsibility must be excited and properly directed. It may as well be frankly admitted that mere intellectual education does not arm men with the power and disposition to resist the cravings of appetite, or the seductive influence of supposed self-interest. If experience ever settles anything, that has been finally decided by the results of the education of the last half-century. The springs of human action lie either above or below the intellect — either above in the moral and religious nature, or below among the appetites and passions. If the higher nature is not developed, strengthened, and directed, the lower will be certain to secure the mastery, in spite of the veneering and polish which come of the culture of intellect and taste. If public sentiment will not tolerate moral instruction in the public schools, and if teachers are not prepared to give and enforce such instruction, both by principle and conduct, then text-books on the "Effects of Alcohol and Narcotics upon the Human System," though approved · by all the "Boards" in the State, will have little practical value. Children, and those older than children, must, if they are to be moved to action, not only know that a specific indulgence of appetite or a certain course of life results in bodily harm and loss, but they must also feel that the indulgence and course of life involve moral responsibility and guilt.

Charles Lamb, writing out of his own bitter experience, says, "Could the youth, to whom the flavor of his first wine is delicious, look into my desolation, and be made to understand what a dreary thing it is when a man feels himself going down a precipice with open eyes and a passive will,— to see his destruction and to have no power to stop it, and yet to feel it, all the way, emanating from himself; to perceive all goodness emptied out of him, and yet not to be able to forget a time when it was otherwise, — to bear about the piteous spectacle of self-ruin," he might be saved from entering upon the downward path. In this extract Lamb touches the core of the matter. Alcohol destroys the power of the will, and thus destroys the vital essence of all true manhood. Of the confirmed inebriate there is little hope: the foundation is terribly shattered, if not absolutely swept away. "When he would do good, evil is present with him." He is wretched, and is an object of pity. But he is also guilty — guilty of slow and deliberate suicide. Humanity, religion, patriotism bid us, by all possible means, save the young — save them from dishonor, degradation, crime, insanity, idiocy.

CHAPTER XIV.

TOBACCO AND OTHER NARCOTICS AND INSANITY.

The consumption of tobacco has gone on steadily increasing for many years. Old men and young men use it; boys, and even children, use it. Clergymen, lawyers, doctors, teachers — indeed, "all sorts and conditions" of people unite in worshiping at the shrine of "the weed." It is chewed, and smoked, and snuffed. It is presented in forms enticing and forms disgusting.

Recent investigations have proved that a considerable portion of the boys in many of our public and other schools use tobacco either habitually or occasionally. In some schools fully forty per cent. have begun to acquire the habit of either chewing or smoking. In not a few cases they commence the practice as early as at eight years of age.

It produces little effect to declaim against this use of tobacco on moral or economical grounds. To say that the habit is offensive and filthy is only repeating what has been reiterated a thousand times to no purpose. If this pernicious habit is to be checked, other considerations and arguments must be employed; and it is a hopeful omen that the influence of tobacco upon the physical organism is beginning to attract serious attention.

Its immediate effects upon one not habituated to its uses are well known. "A biting sensation, more or less marked, in the mucous membrane of the mouth, tongue, and throat, a feeling of warmth and faintness, nausea, vomiting, and headache, presently a coolness of the skin, perspiration on the forehead, hurried respiration, and feeble action of the heart," are symptoms familiar to · observation and experience. It is well established that the nicotine of tobacco, one of the most active of poisons, acts directly upon the brain and nervous system, producing at first a partial paralysis.

Fortunately, or perhaps unfortunately, for the physical vigor of the race, the system in maturity has power to adjust itself to this poison, and the peculiar effects just alluded to soon cease to appear. In place of these a soothing and pleasing influence is felt, which probably comes from a very slight paralysis of the nerves, just sufficient to allay the sense of discomfort and irritation produced by exhaustion or other causes. The power of resistance and adjustment is so great in the adult body that the moderate use of tobacco may be continued for a long time with little observable harm. The excessive use, even in the adult, soon yields a prolific harvest of evil; and the poor victim of artificial appetite is compelled to choose between the pain of breaking off a habit not easily broken and premature death, or physical, if not mental, imbecility.

It is hardly possible to exaggerate the pernicious effects of the constant use of tobacco upon the young. The immature brain, nerves, and muscles have little power of resistance or adjustment. The inevitable consequence is that the organs of the body do not attain their normal growth or reach a vigorous maturity. The boy who commences the habitual use of tobacco in any form at eight years of age, never becomes the man he might have been. His vitality has been sapped and weakened. The result is a general flabbiness, to employ a word more expressive than elegant, of the whole man, mental and moral as well as physical. Both the intellectual and moral powers are less active, keen, and sensitive, than they otherwise would have been.

So thoroughly has this been proved that in France and Germany legal enactments have been made forbidding the use of tobacco by pupils in many of their schools. During some years its use has not been allowed in the naval and military schools of the United States. To say nothing of individual welfare, the public interests demand that effectual restrictions be put upon the sale of tobacco, in any form, to young boys, and that some effectual means be devised to prevent its use by the pupils in our public schools. It is not so much a question of morals as of manhood; patriotism is as much concerned as purity; the State has a deeper interest than even the family. It is time, certainly, that the pulpit and the desk, the preacher and the teacher, were purified from the sight and smell of tobacco; if not for moral and religious considerations, then for the sake of physical manhood and political economy.

 It is not claimed that the use of tobacco is, in any large number of cases, the direct cause of insanity. Indirectly, and associated with other causes, it is responsible for much mental as well as physical suffering. It inflicts its harm, chiefly, by preventing the proper maturing of the system, especially the nervous system, and by reducing its tone and vigor, and thus exposing it, with weakened powers of defense, to the attacks of other enemies. While it may not, to any considerable extent, directly originate mental disease, it certainly breaks down the barriers, opens the doors, and invites such disease to enter, and makes its progress more easy, sure, and deadly. It acts the part of a pretended friend, who does not, indeed, set fire to your house, but who does surreptitiously remove all means of extinguishing the flames.

Moreover, by the laws of heredity, the effects of the habitual use of tobacco go beyond the immediate victim and the present generation, and entail a load of ills and a possible burden of woes upon posterity. An unstable physical and mental organization is a sad patrimony to bequeath to one's children, and a fearful price to pay for a little temporary gratification of an unnatural appetite.

While speaking thus plainly and emphatically of the evils resulting from the habitual use of tobacco, more particularly to the young, I wish to guard against a possible misapprehension. Nothing is gained, even to a good cause, by exaggeration. The harmful effects of tobacco are bad enough, are surely alarming, but they are not to be compared to those resulting from the use of alcohol. It is, in my opinion, most unwise to confuse and mislead by denouncing both with equal zeal and violence. Alcohol has no peer in capacity and power to work damage to all the interests of humanity. Intemperance begets and perpetuates a greater and more hideous brood of human ills than any other habit, unless it be that of sexual license and impurity.

8

Between the offspring of these kindred monsters a choice would be difficult. Let them enjoy their unenviable pre-eminence.

Of other narcotics opium, of which morphine is the most essential principle, is the most common and the most important in its relations to mental disease. In limited quantities and under certain conditions, opium and morphine produce a species of enticing and pleasurable intoxication. The eater or smoker revels in delightful day-dreams and wondrous flights of fancy. But the "opium habit" is of the most dangerous character. It is seductive, alluring, and fascinating. It seems to cast a fatal spell over its victim, and drags him slowly, but steadily and surely, down to degradation and ruin, physical, intellectual, and moral. The power of self-control and self-direction is soon lost, and the ability to resist the raging demands of unnatural appetite utterly disappears. The natural sensibilities are blunted, and moral distinctions gradually fade away. The habitual user of opium becomes a pitiable wreck, driven hither and thither by the demon which he has himself evoked.

Samuel Taylor Coleridge affords an illustrious example of the depth of misery and helplessness into which a man may be plunged by this terrible habit. For fifteen years he is reported to have been its slave. He made, De Quincey says, "prodigious efforts to deliver himself from this thraldom; and went so far, at one time, as to hire a man for the express purpose, and armed with the power of resolutely interposing between himself and the door of any druggist's shop." A contest actually took place between Coleridge and this "external conscience," who proved faithful to his trust. What an abdication of all manhood is indicated by such a condition! And yet Coleridge, when master of himself, was one of the most brilliant men of his time. Saddest of all, his son Hartley inherited the weakness of the father, and wasted life, as he himself says, "in the woful impotence of weak resolve."

The use of opium in some form is said to have greatly increased in this country within the last few years. The importation in 1881 was 85,075 pounds; in 1883 it amounted to 298,152 pounds. The "opium habit" is probably more common among women than among men, though it is not by any means confined to females. A druggist in one of our cities is reported to have said, "Hundreds of ladies belonging to the best families in the city are addicted to the habit, but the number of men is comparatively small." It is to be hoped that this is a libel upon the women of that city. If true, the accommodations for imbeciles will need to be greatly enlarged in our asylums at an early day. The quantity of morphine taken by persons long accustomed to its use is almost incredible. A dealer in drugs states, "There are women in this city who take enough morphine in a day to kill half a dozen people unaccustomed to it. I have in mind a lady who began coming to my store about five years ago. She began buying packages of fifty cents' worth.   She is now an imbecile, and consumes ten dollars' worth in two months.   There is no such thing as a maximum dose. There are numbers of frail women among my customers, each of whom can take enough morphine at one dose to kill the strongest man in the city."

Such excessive indulgence brings loss of regular and natural appetite, derangement of the organs of digestion, torpor of the intellectual and moral faculties, hallucinations, and confirmed and degrading disease of both body and mind.   If the use of this drug continues to increase, it will obviously be the duty of the civil authorities to interfere, in some vigorous way, with its importation and sale.   The duty of parents, teachers, and others who understand the use and influence of opium, is sufficiently clear.   The young, the weak, and the ignorant are entitled to protection from the danger of contracting a habit whose evil influence can hardly be over-estimated.

CHAPTER XV.

INHERITED TENDENCIES AND INSANITY.

Among my acquaintances and friends are several excellent persons who live constantly under a dark shadow.   In some cases a parent, in other cases a more remote ancestor, suffered from insanity, perhaps died in an asylum.   They have read the recent discussions upon "heredity" and "environment," and are fully persuaded that they are cursed with a fatal inheritance. This idea disquiets them by day and haunts them by night. It is like a perpetual nightmare or an ever-present skeleton. It tends to destroy happiness, to paralyze energy, and, worst of all, to bring upon them the very evil which they so much dread. If possible, I should be glad to present some considerations which might help to dispel the shadow that hangs over individuals of this class. More than anything else, they need courage and grounds upon which to predicate a reasonable hope of escaping the fate impending, as they believe, over them.

Upon this subject of transmitted and inherited tendencies no one except a specialist is qualified to speak with authority. I shall not presume to place any reliance upon the lessons of my own observation in a matter of this sort. I shall, therefore, borrow freely and literally the opinions of those who are competent to instruct.

The doctrine of heredity, in its general form, is not new. A law has always been recognized "by which all beings endowed with life tend to repeat themselves in their descendants." It is not a recent discovery that, "in transmitting the germ of life, parents transmit to their children their own resemblance, physical, mental, and moral; the children are a part of ourselves; it is our flesh, our blood, our souls, our examples, our lessons, our passions, which relive in them." Physical features reappear generation after generation. Intellectual peculiarities live on through many successive fathers and sons. Moral traits appear over and over again. Deformities, weaknesses, idiosyncrasies, and morbid tendencies are also, by the same law, transmitted. All these facts have been understood for ages by intelligent observers. Cultivators of plants and breeders of animals have turned such knowledge to profitable account. They have learned that even special and apparently accidental variations from the normal type may also be transmitted and rendered more or less permanent by the law of inheritance.

Recently, however, there has been a tendency on the part of writers upon "social science" to attach more importance to the law of heredity in its applications to the human race, and to emphasize, if not to exaggerate, its influence. The purpose which these authors desired to accomplish was a laudable one, and one to which the public mind needed to be directed. They have abundantly proved that diseased tendencies of the worst description are propagated from parents to children, and that by this means the most fearful evils are constantly and rapidly increasing. It has been shown, beyond all question, that the drunkard, whether habitual or only occasional, entails upon his posterity an inheritance of woes positively frightful to contemplate. In no other disease are the hereditary influences so fatally sure as in alcoholism.

Dr. Morel says:

"Defective nerve-power and an enfeebled, debilitated *morale*
form the favorite legacy of inebriates to their offspring. Some of
the circle, generally the daughters, may be nervous and hysteri-
cal; others, generally sons, are apt to be feeble and eccentric,
and to fall into insanity when an unusual emergency takes place.
That the impairment of the bodily or mental faculties arises from
intemperance of one or both heads of the family is demonstrated ,
by the healthfulness and intellectual vigor of the children born
while the parents were temperate, contrasted with the sickliness
and mental feebleness of their brothers and sisters born after the
parent or parents became intemperate. The most distressing
aspect of the heredity of alcohol is the transmitted narcotic or
insatiable craving for drink,— the dipsomania of the physician,—
which is every day becoming more and more prevalent."

It is stated upon apparently .good authority that
"the records of asylums all indicate that the tendency
to insanity, in some of its forms, is one of those most likely
to be inherited. It is thought that more than one half
of the admissions to English asylums present evidence
of an inherited taint. The same is probably true in
reference to admissions to asylums in the United
States."

It would be strange if statements of this kind,
fortified by statistics of the most formidable character,
and left without explanation or qualification, did not
produce a deep and depressing influence upon the
minds of those who have reason to suppose such a
taint to run in their blood.

This depressing effect is deepened by the further
application of the doctrine of heredity to the depraved,
vicious, and criminal classes. Transmitted tendencies

and environment are made responsible for a very large percentage of all violations of law and order. Theft and robbery, assault and murder, larceny and lechery, flow concealed in the veins, and only wait provocation and opportunity to make themselves manifest.

Undoubtedly there is a large measure of truth in this view, enough to demand for it the careful consideration of the law-making and law-administering powers, as well as of the common citizen and practical philanthropist. But it is quite possible to draw from this doctrine deductions and inferences of the most unfortunate and harmful nature. Man may be reduced to a mere automaton, impelled to act by forces over which he has no control, the mere slave of inherited tendencies and of external surroundings. Powerless to resist, unable to direct, why should yielding incur guilt or be visited with penalties? Machines are not blamed or punished; and, under this theory followed to an easily reached extreme, the human being becomes a mere piece of animated mechanism. Moral distinctions vanish; right and wrong are obsolete and meaningless terms; virtue and vice are fictions of the imagination. So-called bad men are only weak, not wicked; unfortunately organized, not morally culpable; victims of heredity, and not of self-created habits of evil-doing.

This is a phase of scientific fatalism toward which a class of very honest and zealous reformers will find themselves drifting, unless we are allowed to suppose that some conservative and preservative forces exist in

men and in society which are strong enough to resist,
at some point, inherited tendencies to physical and
moral degradation. I am confident that such forces do
exist. I believe that heredity itself, when rightly
understood and correctly interpreted, is a conservative and not a destructive force. The normal condition of any organism is a state of health, and not of
disease. The native, natural tendency is to perpetuate
the normal condition, unless the whole organism is
totally corrupted, vitiated beyond all possibility of
restoration. In this case, by a merciful provision of
nature, death soon intervenes, and the ruined individual or family or race disappears.

Except in such extreme cases, inherited physical tendencies can to a considerable extent, at least, be successfully resisted and overcome by persistent and intelligent efforts. The same is true of transmitted intellectual and moral traits. It is not affirmed that the
task will be an easy one, or that the struggle will be
of short duration; but it is most emphatically affirmed
that every sane man's consciousness revolts against the
imputation that he is a mere automaton, destitute of
all self-directing power. We seem to ourselves, at any
rate, to have a form of mental activity called choice,
and to be able to give "preponderance to motives."
We are able, consciously and voluntarily, to check
some impulses and to yield to others, to give to one
motive more weight than to another. We feel, when
in a state of ordinary mental and moral soundness,

that we are not irresistibly impelled to pursue a certain course or to do certain things. It is easy for a theorist to assert that we are cheated by what we call consciousness; but it is not easy to discover by what means, or by what course of argument, such an assertion can be satisfactorily established. There is nothing behind or below consciousness in the soul to which an appeal can be made. Its decisions are of necessity final in all matters of this kind.

Of the influence of this specious form of fatalism, Dr. Carpenter says:

"I can imagine nothing more paralyzing to every virtuous effort, more withering to every noble aspiration, than that our children should be brought up in the belief that their characters are entirely formed by *heredity* and *environment;* that they *must* do whatever their respective characters impel them to do; that they have no other power of resisting temptations to evil than such as may *spontaneously* arise from the knowledge they have acquired of what they ought or ought not to do; that if this motive proves too weak they can do nothing of themselves to intensify and strengthen it; that the notion of 'summoning their resolution,' or 'bracing themselves for the conflict,' is altogether a delusion; that, in fine, they are in the position of a man who is floating down stream without oars, towards a dangerous cataract, and can only be rescued by some external power."

How this doctrine weighs "like an incubus" on the soul is well stated by J. S. Mill in his autobiography. He says, "I felt as if I was scientifically proved to be a helpless slave of antecedent circumstances; as if my character and that of all others had been formed for us by agencies beyond our control, and was *wholly out of our own power.*"

This is essentially the condition in which some of the persons of whom I have spoken believe themselves to be. They are scientifically proved to be helpless, "fore-ordained" to a fate which horrifies them, but against which it is worse than useless to struggle. It is hardly necessary to say that I am not a believer in this crushing species of "fore-ordination." This is not the teaching of the doctrine of heredity, interpreted by reason or consciousness.

Even J. S. Mill, on reflection, reached another conclusion. "I saw," he says, "that though our characters are formed by circumstances, *our own desires can do much to shape those circumstances;* and that what is really inspiriting and ennobling in the doctrine of Free-will, is the conviction that we have real power over the formation of our own characters; that our will, by influencing some of our circumstances, can modify our future habits and capacities of willing."

Mr. Mill here touches the heart of the whole matter. In spite of all theorizing, we feel that the will, unless utterly destroyed by the most vicious and degrading habits, has some self-directing power; that we can modify and, to some extent, control circumstances; that we are not doomed to drunkenness because an ancestor has unfortunately been an inebriate, or to insanity because a father or mother, or some remote relative, has suffered from mental disease. It is freely conceded that hidden tendencies course in our veins; that a taint vitiates our blood; that concealed enemies lurk to pounce upon us at some unguarded moment; that constant watchfulness is the only guaranty of safety; — but we are not utterly helpless, mere floating wrecks, with no power of self-direction and no possibility of escape from the dangers which threaten us.

I recall in my native neighborhood, in a country town of New England, two families, in one of which the father was frequently and habitually intoxicated, and in the other the father was habitually a constant and hard drinker. In both families the mother was of most excellent character and habits. Each family had a half-dozen children, a majority of them boys, nearly all of whom grew up to manhood, and several of whom are still living quite advanced in years. Not one child in either family has been addicted to the use of intoxicating drinks, nor has any one, so far as I have been able to learn, suffered from any form of mental disease. It is true that some of the children were born before the fathers had fallen into the confirmed habit of inebriety; but not all of them. The latest-born inherited less vigorous physical constitutions, but otherwise there was no difference in character. Examples can be recalled in abundance, where children have followed in the unhappy footsteps of their besotted parents. I have adduced this one to show that such following is not a "fore-ordained" necessity; that there is an innate power by which one can, if he will, overcome inherited inclinations and dispositions.

This view is confirmed by the testimony of a multitude of competent witnesses among specialists and physicians generally.

Dr. Parish says:

"The law of heredity recognizes periods of limitation, as a necessity for the continuance of the race. If it were not for such a law, and the degenerative process were to be continued, without deviation or exhaustion, the reproductive powers would sooner or later terminate, and the race become extinct.

"It is evident that the individual who is conscious of an inherited tendency to alcoholic excess, may do much to modify, if not to control its force, by placing himself under such conditions of living as will tend to increase his constitutional vigor in the direction in which it is most needed. A person coming into the world with a tendency to pulmonary consumption will, as soon as he knows it, begin to correlate himself with the most favorable conditions of climate, occupation, etc., that the progress of the morbific element within him may be arrested, if possible, and that the normal forces that are antagonistic to this manifestation of disease may be strengthened. The same is true of other disorders.

"A person with a direct hereditary taint for insanity may pursue a course of life, under professional guidance, which will secure him against a public exhibition of his infirmity, with more certainty than a person with an alcoholic diathesis can be kept from indulgence and exposure. In the former there is no physical craving to overcome, no struggle with an internal and positive demand, which, strong and imperious itself, is rendered more so by the allurements of social and the attractive displays of public life. All that is required in case of the insane tendency is, in the very outset, to submit to intelligent guidance as to mental and physical hygiene, so as to preserve a normal equipoise."

Dr. Hitchcock, writing upon the fearful "Entailments of Alcohol," says:

"Can a young man who, from some taint of blood, has inherited from his parents or ancestors that morbid desire for stimulants, be secured from this brood of evils? Yes, if the taint of blood is not so strong as to wholly enervate the will; but he only by total abstaining. And is it not possible that by so doing, and by intermarrying with a person in whose blood there is no such taint, he may do much towards eliminating that taint from his descendants?"

That which must be done in respect to the "taint" of alcohol, can more surely be done in respect to the less terrible taint of insanity.

Dr. Van Deusen writes:

"To have an inherited capacity for mental disease is one thing, and to have a parent or relative who may have been insane may be quite another. The somewhat general impression that the child of a parent who has been insane, is quite sure to suffer in the same manner, *is by no means correct;* it is often mischievous, in suspending over the child a painful and ever-present apprehension, generally morbid in its influence, and of service, perhaps, when it leads to a judicious and healthful system of development and discipline, and more carefully regulated habits of life. It is evident enough that there can be no possible direct transmission to offspring in the case of a parent who, many years after the birth of a child, from purely physical causes, may suffer from an attack of mental disease.

"In this connection it may be of some advantage to suggest to the friends of insane parents the importance of preventing intimate and protracted association with their children in the early years of their development. The sadly depressing effect of such association has very frequently been demonstrated, especially in case of an insane mother and her daughter. The fact of the existence of such an influence is too important to be disregarded."

"Our experience leads to the conclusion that, (1), about one-third of all presented for treatment have immediate relatives who have been insane; (2), that most forms of mental disease are equally curable, whether the patient has sane or insane relatives; (3), that individuals of ordinarily good mental and physical constitution, in whom recovery is perfect, are less likely to have a second attack; while, (4), those who inherit an unhealthy organization will probably suffer from subsequent attacks."

Dr. Hurd says:

"In many instances persons possessing susceptible nervous organizations suffer much unnecessary apprehension because an immediate relative has been insane, when the fact may not have any bearing upon their own prospect of developing insanity. The insanity of old age or of the climacteric period can not be regarded as transmissible.

"What does an insane parent transmit to his offspring? In a vast majority of cases there is transmitted only a *predisposition* to mental disease; mental disease itself is not transmitted, but an impressible mental organization which, under favoring circumstances, is prone to take on diseased action. The inheritance of a predisposition to mental disease *does not affect unfavorably the prospect of recovery* in case of attack.

"Insanity is not invariably developed where a predisposition exists. The person who inherits such predisposition should form careful habits of living. Excesses should be avoided; everything which produces mental strain or worry should be scrupulously shunned, and the individual should, as far as possible, be contented to lead a quiet life, subjected to the fewest possible disturbing influences."

Such testimony ought to relieve, in good measure, those who may have been unduly anxious on account of some real or supposed inherited tendency. At the same time, the imperative necessity of taking all possible precaution against uncalled-for exposure to physical exhaustion, or nervous and mental excitement, should be impressed upon them and upon their friends.

CHAPTER XVI.

INSANITY AND CRIME.

It will appear to border closely on presumption for one who is neither a lawyer, physician, or a specialist, to express with much freedom opinions touching the responsibility of the insane and the treatment by the courts of persons charged with crime and defended on·the plea of mental disease.

It is freely conceded that only those who have made insanity a subject of profound study, and have had opportunities to observe, for protracted periods and under favorable conditions, the conduct of the insane and the peculiar and varied manifestations of disordered mental and moral activity, are fully competent to prescribe and apply tests of responsibility in cases where misconduct or criminal acts are laid to the charge of persons suspected of mental unsoundness. The question of responsibility in such cases is confessedly surrounded with very great and grave difficulties, and justice and humanity unite in demanding of those who are to give answer to it the utmost candor, the most unwearied patience, and a willingness to be instructed even at the risk of acknowledging previous ignorance.

The problem is rendered more perplexing to the ordinary observer, and its solution is made more

hopeless, by the fact that in cases which come before
the courts specialists, apparently equally well-informed and equally well-intentioned, give opinions
and reach conclusions of a widely different character.
One is very forcibly reminded of the antiquated
adage, "When doctors disagree." The confusion is
still further confounded by contentions, charges, and
counter-charges, between the medical and legal professions. The doctors propose one standard of
responsibility and the lawyers insist upon another.
In the din which often arises the common people not
unnaturally conclude that nothing is positively
known about the matter, and fall back contentedly
and complacently upon the traditional notions which
they have inherited from the ignorance and prejudice
of the past. Juries composed of such people, and
perhaps unconsciously influenced by the passions and
sentiments of the hour, alternate in their verdicts
from severity which borders on barbarism to leniency
which more than borders on impunity to disorder and
crime. In one case a man obviously insane is condemned to death, while in another case a criminal
worthy of the severest punishment is set free on the
convenient but shallow plea of "emotional insanity."
The height of absurdity was reached, and the mock-
ery of legal forms was completed, when a jury
declared, in substance, "We find that the accused
was entirely sane the moment before and the moment
after the act [deliberate killing] was committed, but

9

we have doubt of his sanity at the instant when the deed was done." The prisoner was allowed the benefit of the doubt, and turned loose into the community to repeat the act, if a similar impulse should seize upon him under some real or supposed provocation.

Under all the circumstances it seems to me to be within the limits of forgiveness if an untrained layman, a mere common observer, should venture the expression of an opinion or the utterance of some inquiries. I can not resist the impression that in the treatment of insanity and the insane, the legal profession and the courts of law have not kept abreast of the general progress of the age. The impression may be a false one, but it is, nevertheless, deeply fixed. The scenes connected with the trial of the assassin of President Garfield, and scenes connected with the trials of less famous criminals, have served to intensify this into a nearly settled opinion. The opinion or belief of an obscure individual is of little importance, but if it should be true that the same impression is fastening itself upon the minds of the great body of fairly intelligent citizens, the opinion, or belief, becomes of consequence to the law-making and law-administering powers. Trials can not degenerate into broad farces and courts into objects of ridicule and contempt without serious danger to the highest interests of the whole body of the people, to say nothing of the safety of the unfortunate or the criminal. It may be of service here, to the unprofessional reader, to borrow some statements of the principles and rules by which the courts have been, and still are, governed in the administration of justice in cases involving, or supposed to involve, the question of insanity.

In the seventeenth century, Lord Hale, one of the most learned and upright judges of England, said:

"There is a partial insanity and a total insanity. Some persons that have a competent use of reason in respect of some subjects, are yet under a particular dementia in respect of some particular discourses, subjects, or applications; — or else it is partial in respect of degrees; and this is the condition of very many, especially melancholy persons, who for the most part discover their defects in excessive fears and griefs, and yet are not wholly destitute of the use of reason; and this partial insanity seems not to excuse them in the committing of any offence for its matter capital; for, doubtless, most persons that are felons of themselves and others are under a degree of partial insanity when they commit these offences. It is very difficult to define the invisible line that divides perfect and partial insanity; but it must rest upon circumstances duly to be weighed by judge and jury, lest, on the one side, there be a kind of inhumanity towards the defects of human nature, or, on the other side, too great an indulgence given to great crimes."

It is assumed in this declaration that an insane man may properly and justly be punished for any acts committed, provided his insanity is partial and not total. Under this principle a large majority, indeed nearly all, of those charged with crimes and defended on the plea of mental disease, would be classed among the partially insane. At a later period, in 1723, the doctrine of Lord Hale was expressed in plainer language by Justice Tracy. He said:

"It is not every kind of frantic humour, or something unaccountable in a man's actions, that points him out to be such a madman as is exempted from punishment. It must be a man that is totally deprived of his understanding and memory, and doth not know what he is doing, no more than an infant, than a brute or a wild beast; such a one is never the object of punishment."

This was very naturally known as "the wild beast theory."

The unprofessional mind is perplexed to discover that the same rule in relation to insanity did not apply to both criminal and civil cases. A person might be adjudged unfit to take proper care of himself, or to manage his business affairs, to make bargains or to dispose of property, and yet be hanged for murder or imprisoned for theft. This is expressly stated by Chief Justice Mansfield in a remarkable trial which occurred in 1812. He says, "Upon the authority of the first sages in the country, and upon the authority of the established law in all times, which has never been questioned, that although a man might be incapable of conducting his own affairs, he may still be answerable for his criminal acts, if he possess a mind capable of distinguishing right from wrong." There is in this declaration a slight advance from the doctrine of Lord Hale. Such knowledge as the infant or the brute may be supposed to have, is exchanged for the somewhat higher knowledge of "right and wrong."

Yet most unfortunately this knowledge is of a general and not of a specific character. That is, the person is held responsible if he can distinguish right from wrong in ordinary affairs, no matter how confused or warped his judgment may be in respect to the crime with which he is charged. Lord Mansfield himself, in speaking of a case in which a patient, laboring under the delusion of having been injured, takes revenge by violence, says, "If such a person were capable, in other respects, of distinguishing right from wrong, there was no excuse for any act of atrocity which he might commit under this description of derangement. It must be proved beyond all doubt that at the time he committed the atrocious act, he did not consider that murder was a crime against the laws of God and nature." Very few, if any, insane homicides could escape conviction for murder in a court governed by this rule. The overmastering power of a delusive idea, driving one on over the opposing forces of knowledge, judgment, conscience, and natural affection, is not recognized. The point upon which the whole question of responsibility depends has thus far eluded the legal mind. In commenting upon the doctrine of Lord Mansfield, Dr. Ray says:

"That the insane mind is not entirely deprived of this power of moral discernment, but on many subjects is perfectly rational and displays the exercise of a sound and well-balanced mind, is one of those facts now so well established, that to question it would only display the height of ignorance and presumption. The first result, therefore, to which the doctrine leads is, that no man can successfully plead insanity in defence of crime; because it can be said of no one who would have occasion for such a defence, that he was unable in any case to distinguish right from wrong. . . The purest minds can not express greater horror and loathing of various crimes than madmen often do, and from precisely the same causes. Their abstract conceptions of crime, not being perverted by the influence of disease, present its hideous outlines as they ever were in the healthiest condition; and the disapprobation they express at the sight arises from sincere and honest convictions. The *particular* criminal act, however, becomes divorced in their minds from its relations to crime in the abstract; and being regarded only in connection with some favorite object which it may help to obtain, and which they see no reason to refrain from pursuing, is viewed, in fact, as of a highly laudable and meritorious nature. Herein, then, consists their insanity, not in preferring vice to virtue, in applauding crime and deriding justice, but in being unable to discern the essential identity of nature between a particular crime and all other crimes, whereby they are led to approve what, in general terms, they have already condemned. It is a fact, not calculated to increase our faith in the 'march of intellect,' that the very trait peculiarly characteristic of insanity has been seized upon as a conclusive proof of sanity in doubtful cases; and thus the infirmity that entitles one to protection, is tortured into a good and sufficient reason for completing his ruin."

At a later period the English judges declared that " to establish a defence on the ground of insanity, it must be clearly proved that, at the time of committing the act, the party accused was laboring under such a defect of reason from disease of the mind as not to know the nature and quality of the act he was doing, or, if he did know it, that he did not know he was doing what was wrong."

This is a long stride in advance of the rule that an accused person is to be held responsible for his acts, however insane he may obviously be, provided he has a general knowledge of right and wrong. Unfortunately the doctrine enunciated in the statement quoted was seriously modified by subsequent rules, and was made less favorable to the ends of justice. An English writer of high standing says of trials in the English courts:

"It is notorious that the acquittal or conviction of a prisoner, when insanity is alleged, is a matter of chance. Were the issue to be decided by tossing up a shilling, instead of by the grave procedure of a trial by court, it could hardly be more uncertain. The less insane person sometimes escapes, while the more insane person is sometimes hanged; one man laboring under a particular derangement is acquitted at one trial, while another having an exactly similar form of derangement is convicted at another trial. No one will be found to uphold this state of things as satisfactory, although there is great difference of opinion as to the cause of the uncertainty; the lawyers asserting that it is owing to the fanciful theories of medical men who never fail to find insanity where they earnestly look for it, the latter protesting that it is owing to the absurd and unjust criterion of responsibility which is sanctioned by the law."

The same language might be used in describing the state of affairs in the United States and probably in all civilized countries. Surely it may be pardonable to suggest that such a condition of things is humiliating in the extreme, if not positively disgraceful to the intelligence of two of the learned professions. Happily the administration of law is often better than the law itself, and innocence, exposed to injustice by the letter of the statute or the rule, is protected by the intervention of a court where the presiding justice has the humanity and courage to set aside the authority of technical definitions and antiquated rulings, and to decide in accordance with the teachings of modern science and with the spirit of an age more humane than that of Lord Hale or Lord Mansfield. But the sense of right and justice in individual judges is usually powerless, under existing laws and rules of proceeding, to prevent injustice or to correct erroneous verdicts. Some radical changes are needed. Only thoroughly trained specialists in the law and in mental disease are competent to suggest the details of such changes; but it may be allowable for any one whose attention has been turned in that direction, to make inquiries or even to express an opinion. Such inquiries and expressions may help towards the formation of a public sentiment which shall demand improvements in the laws and in the methods of their administration.

In cases of crime in which insanity is claimed as a ground of defence, ought not the question of sanity or insanity to be examined and determined entirely apart from the question of the criminal act itself?

Let the trial of one question, the question of insanity, either precede or follow the trial as to the act or crime charged. Let the tribunal be one having some fitness for the examination and decision of such a question, and not an ordinary jury. It is no imputation upon the intelligence or honesty of the members of an ordinary jury to say that they have no competency for the determination of such a question. Insanity is either itself a disease, or it is the result of a disease, as much as diphtheria or typhoid fever. A jury of farmers, mechanics, or merchants, would hardly be expected to decide satisfactorily whether an alleged case of typhoid fever were that disease or some other. It is hardly less absurd to set the same men to determine whether an act of brutal assault is the offspring of a violent insane delusion, or of an ungovernable feeling of ill-will and revenge.

Should not a court, when it is claimed that a prisoner is insane, or was insane at the time the offence was committed, be authorized, and under some circumstances be required, to summon a small jury of men familiar with all forms and peculiarities of mental disorders, and to submit to them the simple question of responsibility? Is the prisoner of unsound mind? and, if so, is the unsoundness of such a character as to render him legally irresponsible for the supposed crime? In many cases this question could be determined before any other proceedings were had, and if the irresponsibility were

clearly established, no further trial would be necessary. In this way, in many cases, much time, great
expense, and often unwholesome excitement would be
saved, and the ends of justice would be easily and
promptly attained.

In cases where insanity is obscure or doubtful,
this jury of experts might be summoned to attend,
observe the prisoner, the witnesses, and the whole
proceedings during the trial as to the fact before the
usual jury, and, in case of conviction, might afterwards render their verdict in respect to sanity and
responsibility. The ordinary jury takes no cogni-
zance of the question of insanity. It considers the
question of guilt or innocence as in any other case,
and that alone.

It is not to be anticipated that this or any similar method of dealing with criminals suspected of
insanity will be immediately adopted. Meanwhile
may we not hope for a less radical, but still an
important improvement in legal practice? As matters now are, in trials involving the plea of insanity,
expert witnesses are employed by both sides, and
these witnesses are examined and cross-examined
very much as other witnesses are. The position is a
humiliating one to intelligent, honorable, and high-
minded gentlemen. The result does not always tend
to further the ends of justice. The spectacle sometimes becomes little less than disgraceful if the advocates happen to be of that peculiar character fre-

quently found in what are known as "criminal lawyers." It will be permitted, even for a very common observer, to affirm that this mode of conducting such trials ought to be changed at once.

When such witnesses are asked to give opinions, they should be invited by the court itself. Questions should be propounded by the court. Interrogations should relate, not merely to supposed and hypothetical cases and conditions, but to the case in hand and to the prisoner at the bar. Paid advocates should stand aside, whether of the prosecution or the defence. The object is not to convict or acquit, but to secure, if possible, exact justice to all parties.

It is difficult to see why so much of reform and improvement might not easily be made. It is evident that the interests of the community would thereby be better guarded, and the insane themselves be put in a position of greater safety.

It is not likely that any single principle can ever be laid down by the courts, or any statement can be made by specialists in the study of mental disease, which shall serve as a practical test of sanity or insanity when applied by ordinary juries, or by unprofessional men in the common relations of life. While it is possible that some characteristics may pertain to all patients suffering from insanity, it is yet probably true that each case exhibits many peculiarities of its own, and must be considered by itself. The responsibility or irresponsibility of each accused man or woman, in whose case insanity is alleged or suspected, must be determined, not by specific rules, but by competent men after the fullest possible investigation of all the conditions, and circumstances, and indications of that individual case.

No more perplexing problem confronts students of moral philosophy and political economy and social science, than the question of the responsibility and proper treatment of, not only the recognized insane when charged with crime, but of that large and growing class which inhabits a sort of borderland, where insanity, and crime, and defective physical and mental organization, and inherited evil tendencies, and vile surroundings, and filthy habits all meet and mingle in one common cesspool of indescribable pollution and degradation. Civilization and society must be defended against the unthrift and marauding depredations of this unfortunate class. Restraints must be imposed, and penalties must be inflicted; but mercy and compassion surely have some place in dealing with this corrupt and corrupting mass of humanity. Restraints and penalties, as usually inflicted, have little tendency to elevate, purify, and reclaim. The field is not an inviting one, but there is need that it be fully explored. To what extent does legal and moral responsibility attach to the members of this class? Can they be, in some way, segregated, and educated, and trained up into decency and manhood? Must we have a horde of criminals propagating itself, warring against society, a constant source of danger, a standing and perpetual menace against good order and prosperity? These and kindred questions are fast becoming of vital importance to the statesman, the philanthropist, and the Christian, and they are crowding themselves forward and demanding some sort of solution.

CHAPTER XVII.

CONCLUDING THOUGHTS.

Increase of Insanity.—The figures of each successive census seem to show an increase in the relative number of the insane in all the States of the Union. The apparent is probably somewhat greater than the actual increase, from the fact that more care has been taken during the last decades to obtain full and trustworthy information in relation to this subject. There is, also, less unwillingness on the part of relatives and friends to admit the existence of mental disease in their families, and to afford facilities for learning the exact truth in respect to persons thus afflicted. Not very far back in the past the feeling prevailed that, in some unexplained way, something of disgrace attached itself to this form of suffering. Under the influence of this feeling men and women put their friends, who had become insane, out of their own sight and the sight of others, as far as possible. They seldom spoke of them. The insane were, in many cases, practically dead and buried. Unless by accident their existence could not be ascertained by public officers.

To a considerable extent this unfortunate impression has been effaced. With other inherited relics of old superstitions it has either entirely disappeared, or, at any rate, is confined mostly to the dark nooks and by-ways of society. Insanity is regarded as a result of physical disease; and this disease carries with it no more of reproach or disgrace than other disorders. It is possible, therefore, to obtain statistics relating to the insane, upon which a fair degree of reliance may be placed.

Another reason for this reported increase readily suggests itself to one at all acquainted with former and present methods of treating the insane. Under the system of neglect and barbarism practiced in not very remote times, all except those of hardy and vigorous constitutions soon died. There was no accumulation in private places of detention, or in public receptacles, of the weak and feeble. The condition of affairs is now entirely different. More humane and wiser treatment lengthens, by many years, the lives of large numbers of incurable patients. A few of the inmates of the Michigan Asylum have been there twenty-five years, and probably the older institutions have patients who have survived for a still longer period. In consequence of this preservation of chronic invalids, the increase in the relative number of the insane, without doubt, appears to be greater than it really is.

But after making all possible reduction from the results of census figures, for the reasons mentioned and for others which might be given, it remains true, beyond reasonable doubt, that mental disease has increased during the last half-century, and is still increasing. The rate of increase, while not such as to give occasion for serious apprehension, is sufficient to challenge attention and to demand a careful examination of probable causes. It is not within my purpose -to enter upon any extended discussion of these causes. Some of them are easy to discover, and have been necessarily touched upon in previous chapters. Others are more obscure, and their profitable discussion would call for knowledge which I can not claim to possess. Too many crude and half-digested theories have already been put forth by persons whose zeal and good intentions have greatly outrun their wisdom · and discretion. One may be pardoned, however, for hesitating to admit that insanity is a necessary product of civilization.

Prevention of Insanity. — The true province of government is to prevent rather than to punish crime. So, it seems to me, the great purpose of medical science and of physicians should be the prevention rather than the cure of disease. This is especially true in respect to insanity. The erection and support of asylums, in addition to institutions of a penal and reformatory character, are imposing heavy burdens upon the community. It is impossible to provide accommodations enough to meet the growing demands. One asylum is hardly completed before another is called for. As a matter of mere economy, to say nothing of the question of humanity, the State could well afford to provide for the most extensive and thorough investigation into the causes and conditions of mental disease, and the means and measures by which it may be prevented. It would be for the economical interests of the State to publish the results of such investigations, and to employ efficient agencies to circulate this information among the people. It is easy to discover difficulties in the way of prosecuting a work of this kind, but they are not insurmountable. It is morally certain that ignorance is responsible for a large percentage of suffering in this as well as in other directions. While waiting for competent authorities to make other and more extended investigations, it will be profitable for us to sum up briefly some of the conclusions already reached, and to make practical use of the lessons which they teach.

Intermarriage of near Relatives, etc.—A very wide diversity of opinion is found, in works of medical and other writers, in respect to consanguineous marriages. Some affirm, with great positiveness, that the effects of such marriages upon offspring are generally, if not always, harmful. Others question, if they do not deny, the correctness of this conclusion. The predominance of testimony, however, is decidedly against the advisability of intermarriage by persons nearly related by blood. If it were certain that the parties to such a union were both perfectly sound in every respect, in body and mind, it might reasonably be expected that the offspring would have no unfortunate physical or mental inheritance. Such cases, if ever found, are very infrequent. The danger is that the husband and wife, coming, at so little remove, from the same stock, will have the same or similar diseased tendencies. In the great majority of instances this will undoubtedly be true. Under such conditions the children can hardly escape inherited tendencies to disease of body, and probably of mind also. Common observation affords abundant confirmation of the unhappy results of such unions. For the sake of posterity, public sentiment, if not statute law, should render marriages of this kind impossible.

But some other marriages are fraught with almost as much of probable danger to offspring as those between persons near of kin. Two individuals with similar and highly nervous organizations incur great risk in forming the marriage relation with each other. They should seek as partners persons of different

10

temperaments and of strong and steady nerves. It is little short of positive madness for those who have inherited an insane tendency to intermarry. Under such circumstances this tendency is much more likely to be fully developed in the parties themselves, and it would be almost a miracle if their children should escape some permanent form of mental unsoundness.

Love is proverbially blind and deaf, and the teachings of wisdom and experience go for nothing when confronted by passion and fancy and personal interest; but it is none the less an imperative duty to use all the means within one's power to enlighten the ignorant, to excite the attention of the heedless, and to warn the wilful and reckless. Some may be saved; some will be saved; though many will doubtless "pass on and be punished," as the foolish have been doing in all the ages. It were better for themselves, for their friends, and for the world, if some individuals should remain even as Paul, unmarried, though for quite another reason. Says Dr. Godding; "I do not expect to recover love from his blindness, but all the more I recognize how far up in 'the glorious procession of saints and martyrs' some souls will hereafter stand whose lives, like their devotions, have been single, whose silent purpose has been that the inherited taint of their blood should die out of the world with them."

Treatment of the Young. — This topic necessarily received some consideration in a previous chapter, but its importance will justify a few additional remarks. Many serious nervous and mental diseases have their origin in early childhood, or in that critical period when childhood verges into maturity. In many cases children are permitted practically to prescribe their own diet. ,Subject to no steady and efficient control, gratified in every caprice for the sake of immediate temporary quiet, they are allowed to eat highly seasoned food and to drink tea and coffee and, perhaps, other more stimulating and exciting liquids. In early youth they are taken into what is called society, are cheated of needed rest and sleep by late hours, and are frequently placed in circumstances calculated to over-tax, in many ways, a delicate and only partially developed physical organization. The brain, and the nervous system generally, are especially liable to receive permanent injury at this period. Precocious children are exposed to additional danger from an unwise and almost unpardonable stimulating of their brain activity by parents and teachers. I am aware that this is merely the repetition of a tale more than "twice-told." Those who have need to receive warning will very likely read and smile, if they read at all, and still believe that such writing is mostly "cant." These are, nevertheless, words of "truth and soberness." "I speak that which I do know, and testify to that which I have seen." I recall the dull, vacant stare of more than one or two patients, mere boys and girls, in the Asylum, whom this criminal folly had transformed from bright, quick, sparkling pets of the household into hopeless imbeciles. This is one of the sins for which there is little room for forgiveness, unless repentance is deep and bitter, and sought with many tears. While teachers are guilty, the largest measure of responsibility and blame in cases of this kind rests upon parents.

It is universally agreed by intelligent witnesses, that the period of approaching puberty is a season of peculiar exposures and danger to girls. I do not write as a physician, but as a father of grown-up daughters, and as an observer of many years in schools and elsewhere. I do not sympathize profoundly with the periodic outcries against school arrangements and requirements which are made responsible for the largest share of the ills which afflict female humanity. Let teachers, and schools, and studies, and examinations bear all the opprobrium which belongs to them — and it is freely conceded that not a little is due to them; yet the homes and mothers and society must consent, however unwilling, to be held responsible for most of the suffering entailed upon maturing girlhood. The demands of society are often more imperative and more exacting than those of the teacher, however unwise the latter may happen to be in his requirements. All parties are in fault, and mutual crimination and recrimination will not "atone for the past nor give proper guaranties for the future."

If the evils produced by bad management at this period were confined to the body, there would be less reason for earnestness and plainness of speech ; but many cases of insanity can be traced pretty directly to unnecessary exposure, unreasonable demands, and improper treatment at this time. Physicians, well-informed mothers, and experienced and trained nurses can give all needed information in respect to this portion of a girl's life. Boys need oversight, restraint, caution, and proper instruction at this period, but their exposure to physical and mental harm is less than that of the sisters in the family. In respect to moral danger, the exposure is probably about equal to both sexes.

General Care of Health. — It is not proposed to encroach, under this topic, upon the province of the medical adviser, in any measure. Some things belong in common to all persons of ordinary intelligence, and especially to those in any profession whose attention has, by force of circumstances, been directed to them.

I am persuaded that one of the most essential conditions of the preservation and enjoyment of good health is not to think too much and too constantly about the matter of health and sickness. This is as true of the mind as of the body, and is of special importance in cases of inherited tendencies. It is a very common saying that under some circumstances "we always find what we look for." If the object of our search does not exist in reality, the imagination will easily create it, oftentimes in fearfully exaggerated form. If one expects his dinner to "set hard" in the stomach, and watches intently for coming discomfort, he will probably not watch in vain. Should something happen to divert his attention for an hour or two from the subject of food and digestion, he may escape all inconvenience and pain. If one expects to find some symptom of mental disorder which a parent may possibly have transmitted, and scrutinizes every thought and feeling, looking at everything in the most unfavorable light, he will probably discover that for which he is waiting, at first only in fancy, but soon in bitter reality. This process of introspection, continued day after day, perhaps month after month, finally turns the action of the mind into the direction of the morbid tendency. The person has brought upon himself the very evil which he feared; and has done this in the most expeditious manner and in accordance with the well-known laws of mental activity. The inclination to "brood" over anticipated feelings is, in some cases, the cause and, in other cases, the consequence of aberration of mind. In either case safety demands that the inclination shall be vigorously and persistently resisted by all the means in one's power. The only effectual resistance is the pre-occupation of the mind by other subjects. To secure this is sometimes extremely difficult, especially if the current of morbid thought and feeling has become thoroughly established. Each individual case has its own peculiarities, and no general rule for treatment can be suggested. The advice of an intelligent student of nervous and mental diseases should be sought in all serious and doubtful cases.

Another condition of mental as well as of physical health is sufficient sleep. Sleeplessness is a signal of danger. If long-continued, it can hardly fail to result in serious harm. The nervous force becomes rapidly exhausted; the power of self-control is weakened, and the mind is easily unbalanced. The human system requires and must have periods of complete repose, and other seasons when relaxation can be secured by interchanging one mode of activity for another. Only in sleep can absolute rest be obtained; and whoever defrauds nature and himself of the requisite hours of sound and refreshing sleep, is sure, in the end, to pay a terrible penalty. Shakespeare's lines are as true as they are familiar:

"Sleep, that knits up the ravell'd sleave of care,
  The death of each day's life, sore labor's bath,
  Balm of hurt minds, great nature's second course,
  Chief nourisher in life's feast."

It is pretty generally agreed that, while no absolute rule can be given, the average time required by the ordinary adult is not less than eight hours of the twenty-four. Some persons need even more, and a few can retain good health with less. The demand of the system for sleep is modified by age and, to some extent, by employments. It was formerly taught that brain-workers could satisfy the wants of nature with fewer hours of sleep than men engaged in mere manual labor. This idea has been abandoned, and it is now universally conceded that vigorous mental activity exhausts the vital force and the nervous energy more than muscular exercise, and calls for a corresponding increase in the time set apart for rest.

The quality of sleep is believed to be of as much importance as the quantity. The most refreshing sleep is that of which memory gives us no account when we are awake,— a quiet, dreamless, unconscious state of complete repose. More, if possible, than others, the student, the teacher, and brain-workers in general, have need of this unconscious and absolute sleep.

The so-called sleep during which one continues the mental work with which he has been occupied during the day and evening, or with which he is excited and harassed by continuous and half-waking dreams, and tormented by dangers and difficulties, brings little real rest, and has little restorative power.

Such a condition, if long permitted, can not fail to produce serious evils. A person suffering in this way should question his habits of life and his methods of work, in order to discover and remove the causes of this unnatural state of body and mind, before they have wrought permanent and irreparable damage.

So far as experience and observation enable me to judge, no general rules of much value can be suggested for "going to sleep." Each individual will require advice suited to his own peculiarities, and to the immediate causes of his sleeplessness, and to the conditions and circumstances by which he is surrounded. Resort to sleep-producing drugs should be had only in extreme cases, and then under the direction of a wise medical adviser.

Under ordinary circumstances few things contribute more to mental health than cheerfulness and proper mental activity. A cheerful, hopeful disposition is so much a native endowment that it may be doubted whether one can have this happy temper unless it has come to him as a blessed inheritance. Observation, however, justifies the conclusion that, by persistent and rightly directed effort, a person may attain to a good degree of this health-giving and health-preserving quality of mind.

If one side of the path along which we are obliged to go day by day, is bordered with flowers and all beautiful things, and the other side with repulsive and disgusting objects, it is within our own power to choose which we will see. It is as easy to look one way as the other. It is as easy to be charmed and delighted as it is to be disgusted and pained. Even if the classes are intermingled upon the same side, it is still largely left for us to determine upon which the the eye shall feast itself. Real human life has much the same possibility of selection; and the choice which one makes goes to determine very largely the habitual tone and spirit of his mind. Some persons insist on seeing and remembering only the disagreeable incidents of a journey, only the faults and foibles of their friends, and only the inconveniences and discomforts of their surroundings. Others have a native or acquired faculty of discovering and treasuring up things just the reverse of these. It is possible to cultivate either of these tendencies, and thus to cultivate cheerfulness or its opposite.

It will not be questioned by any intelligent thinker that proper mental activity must be a condition of mental health as certainly as appropriate physical exercise is a condition of bodily vigor and strength. As surely as an arm unused fails to develop in proportion and harmony with other properly exercised members of the body, and soon becomes practically useless, so surely any unemployed intellectual faculty becomes dwarfed and powerless. Allow all the faculties to lie dormant, or to be exercised only in a dull, tread-mill round of petty duties, into which no change or variety ever comes, every succeeding day being an exact reproduction and repetition of yesterday, and mental life and vigor will, in a majority of cases, gradually become enfeebled, and in some cases the man or woman will become a hopeless, and usually a harmless imbecile. If to this mental stagnation be added hard, continuous, and exhausting physical labor, deprivation of congenial society, and neglect on the part of friends, the process of mental degeneration will be hastened, and the result will be more profound and pitiable wretchedness. Not a few of the inmates of asylums have found their way to these institutions along this cheerless track, in consequence of the ignorance or insensibility of near relatives and friends. Most of these sufferers are women, many of them are wives and mothers. Dr. Stearns gives an illustrative example in the case of a mother of eight children brought by her husband to the asylum of which he was in charge. The husband was at loss to conceive any possible cause for the insanity of his wife. In speaking of her he said, "Her is a most domestic woman, is always doing something for her children; her is *always* at work for us all; *never* goes out of the house, even to church on Sundays; her never goes gadding about at neighbors' houses, or talking from one to another; her always had the boots blacked in the morning; her has been one of the best wives and mothers, and was *always* at home." A more graphic description of mental suicide, if the course of life was altogether voluntary on the part of the wife, or of mental homicide, if the manner of living was compelled, directly or indirectly, by the husband, could hardly be written.

If either physical, or mental, or even moral health is to be preserved, something of variety, of relaxation, of amusement and recreation, must be provided to break up the dull monotony of an unchanging round of daily labors, which come and go with the unbroken regularity of day and night. Every impulse of the soul cries out against this everlasting sameness, and struggles, in some way, to be rid of it as of a frightful nightmare.

Of the many other particulars which might find place under this head, I will, in closing, mention only one: Cultivate a spirit of faith and trust. In the nature of things, as we find them, "offences will come," occasions of distrust, doubt, perplexity. What we know is bounded, on all sides, by that which we do not and can not know fully and positively; we can, at best, only believe and hope; and, in some directions, we find ground merely for conjectures and guesses. It is not difficult to keep one's self in a state of perpetual disquiet and unrest by grasping after that which is quite beyond our reach, by striving to comprehend the incomprehensible, to know the unknowable, and to fathom the unfathomable. Proper mental effort is not to be discouraged, nor is the disposition to search and inquire to be blamed; but while all things may be lawful, some things are inexpedient for individuals of certain temperaments and organizations. When the boundary line of the sure and certain has been reached, it will be safer and better for the most of us to pause, turn back, and rest in the assurance that He, whose care extends to the lilies and the sparrows, will not leave us unprotected. Faith in God and in humanity, trust in Providence and in friends, will often save the mind from wreck and the soul from despair.

> "O Lord! how happy should we be,
> If we could leave our cares to Thee,
> If we from self could rest,
> And feel at heart that One above,
> In perfect wisdom, perfect love,
> Is working for the best.
> Oh! would these heartless souls of ours
> The lesson learn from birds and flowers,
> And learn from self to cease;
> Leave all things to our Father's will,
> And in His mercy trusting still,
> Find, in each trial, peace."

www.ingramcontent.com/pod-product-compliance
Lightning Source LLC
Chambersburg PA
CBHW021109020726
47500CB00003B/676